"If you're planning to tame me with your virile good looks, don't even try."

"It's not you I hope to tame, but the horses."

Bolton continued to gentle the horses with touch and sound, speaking to them in the ancient mystical cadence of his people. He'd never done an interview with a hostile subject, and he didn't plan to start now.

Just as he'd suspected, Virginia's curiosity got the best of her.

"Where did you learn how to do that?"

"I was conceived on a horse."

"What is that language?"

"Athabascan."

Some of the aggressiveness went out of her stance, and she tilted her head to one side as she listened.

"It's beautiful. I'd like to learn it."

"I'll teach you." He turned the full radiance of his smile on her. Virginia felt as if her insides were melting. "I'll teach you many things."

WHAT ARE *LOVESWEPT* ROMANCES?

They are stories of true romance and touching emotion. We believe those two very important ingredients are constants in our highly sensual and very believable stories in the LOVESWEPT line. Our goal is to give you, the reader, stories of consistently high quality that may sometimes make you laugh, sometimes make you cry, but are always fresh and creative and contain many delightful surprises within their pages.

Most romance fans read an enormous number of books. Those they truly love, they keep. Others may be traded with friends and soon forgotten. We hope that each LOVESWEPT romance will be a treasure—a "keeper." We will always try to publish

**LOVE STORIES YOU'LL NEVER FORGET
BY AUTHORS YOU'LL ALWAYS REMEMBER**

The Editors

Loveswept 802

INDISCREET

PEGGY WEBB

BANTAM BOOKS
NEW YORK · TORONTO · LONDON · SYDNEY · AUCKLAND

INDISCREET

A Bantam Book / September 1996

LOVESWEPT and the wave design are registered trademarks of
Bantam Books, a division of Bantam Doubleday Dell Publishing Group,
Inc. Registered in U.S. Patent and Trademark Office and elsewhere.

All rights reserved.
Copyright © 1996 by Peggy Webb.
Cover photo copyright © 1996 by Mort Engel Productions.
Floral border by Joyce Kitchell.
No part of this book may be reproduced or transmitted in any
form or by any means, electronic or mechanical,
including photocopying, recording, or by any
information storage and retrieval system, without
permission in writing from the publisher.
For information address: Bantam Books.

If you purchased this book without a cover you should be aware that
this book is stolen property. It was reported as "unsold and
destroyed" to the publisher and neither the author nor the publisher
has received any payment for this "stripped book."

ISBN 0-553-44565-0

Published simultaneously in the United States and Canada

Bantam Books are published by Bantam Books, a division of Bantam Doubleday Dell Publishing Group, Inc. Its trademark, consisting of the words "Bantam Books" and the portrayal of a rooster, is Registered in U.S. Patent and Trademark Office and in other countries. Marca Registrada. Bantam Books, 1540 Broadway, New York, New York 10036.

PRINTED IN THE UNITED STATES OF AMERICA
OPM   0 9 8 7 6 5 4 3 2 1

DEDICATION

To the precious people of La Joya, Mexico, and my wonderful La Joya teammates, who understand miracles; and to my dear friend, Shirley, who fought with grace and courage against breast cancer—and won.

ONE

"Bolton, I need you to fly down to Mississippi and interview Virginia Haven."

Glenda Williams, editor of *Famous Faces, Famous Places* always got straight to the point.

Bolton's horse was saddled, his camping gear packed, and his dog waiting at the door. Outside his window the White Mountains beckoned. He hesitated only a moment before answering.

"I'm going camping. Send somebody else."

"Who? Luke Farkins? Samuel Bevins? She'd chew them up and spit them out."

"That's not my problem."

"Look, Bolton. Virginia Haven is the hottest writer today. She's just come out with another blockbuster, and every magazine in the country wants a shot at her. But *we* got her. You understand that? She's granting *one* interview, and she's requested you."

Bolton Gray Wolf felt a surge of adrenaline. The

wind sang through the trees in seductive invitation, his horse whinnied, and his dog tugged at his pants' leg. Still, he was being granted an exclusive, and with a woman who was said to be as difficult as she was famous.

"Why me?"

"Don't you ever look in the mirror? Women bare everything they've got when they see you. You're the only photojournalist alive who could make the presidents of Mt. Rushmore give up their secrets."

Bolton laughed. "Does that mean you've finally realized that I'm good?"

"That's what I just said. Come on, Bolton, stop giving me a hard time. You know you love a challenge."

He did. And that's why he unpacked his camping gear, repacked for the muggy Indian summer days of Mississippi, and apologized to his horse and his dog for the inconvenience of a delayed trip.

"We'll go as soon as I get back, fellows. I promise."

His dog Bear forgave him with a thorough tongue bath, and the stallion Lancelot nuzzled his hand and permitted extra stroking. He stayed so long in the stables that he had time to do little more than change his shirt and run a brush through his wild black hair before his date with Janice Blaine.

They'd been seeing each other off and on for three years. Janice was a good friend, an adequate lover, and a darned good schoolteacher.

"Hi, Bolton. You look nice." She always said that, and she always greeted him with a kiss on the cheek.

"So do you."

It was Thursday, spaghetti day. After dinner they sat

Indiscreet

for a while on the front porch holding hands; then when the stars came out they went inside to her small bedroom.

Theirs was a comfortable routine, broken only by her occasional pleas for commitment. Around midnight she stood barefoot at her door and begged him to stay.

"I can't, Janice. I'm flying out early tomorrow, and I have to go home and get the rest of my gear together."

"If we were married, I would help you get all that together, and you could get a good night's rest."

The back of her neck was warm and soft where Bolton rested his hand. Janice was sweet, intelligent, and attractive. She would make a good wife and a great mother.

Tears glittered on her lashes as she took his silence for yet another refusal. He gently kissed them away.

"Don't cry, Janice."

She clutched the lapels of his soft doeskin shirt. "Promise me you'll think about it, Bolton. Promise!"

"I promise."

Bolton wanted marriage and children, and at thirty-five he wasn't getting any younger. Of course, what he really wanted was the kind of marriage his parents had, a union full of fire and magic. Over the years he'd kept hoping to find that kind of love, but it had eluded him.

He thought of all those things on the drive back to his cottage. The dilemma kept him awake most of the night, and on his way to the airport he stopped and bought Janice a ring. If the purchase didn't fill him with joy, at least it gave him a sense of movement into the future.

4

Sometimes a man had to settle for what he could get.

On the plane he forgot about the ring in his pocket. Instead he concentrated on the impending interview. Bolton Gray Wolf prided himself on the excellence of his work, and he wasn't about to go unprepared for an interview with the indomitable Virginia Haven.

The first thing that caught his eye was the stallion. It was an Arabian, strong, surefooted, white as the crest of the snowy egret and as swift as the north winds that whirled down from the White Mountains and overtook the tribal lands in winter. If he could have a chance to ride that horse, then the trip to Mississippi would be well worth his time.

The second thing he noticed was the woman. Tall and lithe, with autumn sunlight streaking her honey-colored hair, she rode like an Apache.

"Last one home is a rotten egg," she called.

The wind caught her laughter and flung it carelessly toward Bolton as if it were something ordinary instead of a rich, husky sound that made his blood sing.

He shaded his eyes to see her better. She was a striking woman, made even more so by the white stallion she rode. The Arabian was a strong-willed, powerful horse, but even at a distance there was no doubt who was in charge.

Over the ridge behind her galloped another Arabian, a perfect match to the one now in a full stretch just beyond the barn where Bolton waited. The rider was

Indiscreet

female, as blond as the first but not quite as tall and definitely not as sure in the saddle.

Could they be twins? He'd been told that Virginia Haven had only one daughter, but the resemblance was so strong that these two had to be sisters.

The second horse raced to catch the first, but both horse and rider were outmatched. In a whirlwind of dust the first Arabian wheeled to a stop just inches from Bolton, and the rider dismounted, her hair flying and her face flushed.

"That's no fair." The second rider came to a stop a few feet away. "You always win, Mother."

Mother! Bolton prided himself on judging a thing right the first time around. He studied Virginia Haven to see what he had missed. Suddenly she wheeled toward the shadows where he was standing.

"Strangers have been shot for less than that," she said.

Virginia Haven strode toward him, leading with her chin in the defiant way of a woman not accustomed to making idle threats. Bolton had been told she hated being interviewed; he hadn't been told she would be openly hostile.

He stepped into the sunlight. "I can assure you I'm not dangerous," he said.

Virginia gave him a frank appraisal that would have made lesser men cringe . . . or blush.

"That remains to be seen," she said.

"Mother!"

Virginia turned to her daughter. "Go on to the house, Candace. I'll handle this."

"Oh, brother." Candace tossed her reins toward her mother, looked as if she might say something else, then changed her mind and headed toward the house.

Nobody in his right mind would call such an imposing layout a mere house. It sat atop a hill in a grove of pecan and oak trees, its wings and gables and porches sprawling in every direction. A garage big enough for at least six cars was attached to the west wing, and a courtyard that might have belonged in Versailles overlooked a six-acre lake.

Bolton was neither intimidated nor impressed. Son of the ever-practical Jo Beth McGill, who preferred canyons to castles, and Colter Gray Wolf, whose taproot was deeply embedded in his Apache homeland, Bolton was a child of nature. For him beauty was the morning sun breaking through the mists of the White Mountains, a fawn wading through a clear brook, an eagle soaring into the vast expanse of Arizona sky. Nature in its untamed state had more appeal to him than fancy houses enclosed with wrought iron fences and protected by security guards.

"I'm Bolton Gray Wolf."

"I know who you are. In the first place, I asked for you, and in the second, you would never have gotten past the front gate without credentials."

Holding on to the reins of the two powerful Arabians as if they were nothing more than Shetland ponies, Virginia started into the stables. "You can wait at the house," she told Bolton as she wheeled past him. "Candace will make you comfortable."

His blood thundered through him like waterfalls af-

Indiscreet

ter a spring thaw. It wouldn't do to let this woman get her bluff in.

"I prefer the stables."

Bolton stepped in close and took the reins of the Arabians.

"My horses don't like to be handled by anybody except me."

Ignoring her, Bolton rubbed the horses and spoke in the ancient mystical cadences of his people. The Arabians proved her wrong by responding to Bolton like children heeding the Pied Piper.

No one had ever dared be so bold with her. Virginia would have put any other man in his place within five seconds flat, but Bolton Gray Wolf was not just any man. Besides looking like something she'd love to eat every morning for breakfast, he had an intriguing aura about him, an aura of mystery and power.

Virginia didn't want to be intrigued. Especially by a photojournalist.

"If you're planning to tame me with your virile good looks, don't even try."

"It's not you I hope to tame, but the horses."

Bolton continued to gentle the horses with touch and sound. He'd never done an interview with a hostile subject, and he didn't plan to start now.

Just as he'd suspected, Virginia's curiosity got the best of her.

"Where did you learn how to do that?"

"I was conceived on a horse."

"What is that language?"

"Athabascan."

Some of the aggressiveness went out of her stance, and she tilted her head to one side as she listened.

"It's beautiful. I'd like to learn it."

"I'll teach you." He turned the full radiance of his smile on her. Virginia felt as if her insides were melting. "I'll teach you many things."

His voice was deep and rich and seductive. Virginia bloomed like a neglected rose that had finally discovered rain and sun and the loving touch of a natural gardener. She welcomed those feelings the way she would old friends who had been gone too long.

Oh, he was dangerous all right, dangerous and gorgeous and delicious . . . and far, far too young.

Virginia shut herself down. Bolton Gray Wolf was off-limits.

"There's nothing you can possibly teach me that I haven't already learned." As she strode toward the house, she flung over her shoulder, "If you want an interview with me, you'd better come on. If not, you can hit the road."

She was halfway across the barn lot when he called her name.

"Virginia . . ." Slowly she turned around. "You forgot about the horses."

It was the first time she'd ever forgotten about her horses. At that moment, she knew beyond a shadow of a doubt that Bolton Gray Wolf would surely break her heart.

TWO

If she had a lick of sense she'd send Bolton Gray Wolf back to Arizona and forget about the interview. That's what she told herself as she walked back toward the stables where he waited with her horses.

His eyes were incredible, as vivid as the wings of a bluebird, and he never took them off her. There was more than professional interest in his stare: There was the hot, bright look of a man aroused. It wasn't something she imagined; it was something she knew.

Her insides quaked like a teenager's.

"What am I getting myself into?" she whispered.

"Did you say something, Virginia?"

"Just talking to myself. Everybody knows writers do that."

"It must be a hazard of the profession, sitting alone in front of a computer."

"Yes, it's a hazard of the profession." She reached for Starfire's bridle, and her hand grazed his. Shock waves that would have felled earthquake-proof buildings went through her.

Another hazard of the profession, she told herself. Constant isolation caused her to go slightly beserk at the touch of a handsome stranger.

Her hands shook as she tried to remove the bridle.

"Here." Bolton covered her hands with his. "Let me help with that."

She should have told him she didn't need help, that she hadn't needed help since Roger had walked out on her fifteen years earlier leaving her with a mountain of debt, a car that wouldn't run in cold weather, and a five-year-old daughter to raise.

But she didn't. It felt so good to have somebody take charge. So damned good. She'd have to be careful, or she'd get to liking it too much.

"In fact, why don't you sit over there and let me take care of the horses?" Bolton nodded in the direction of a bale of hay.

"Is this part of your technique?"

"Technique?"

A hot flush came into her cheeks. She turned her back on him and fanned herself before she sank onto the bale of hay.

"Interviewing technique," she clarified.

His laughter was rich and deep. "No. It's actually a selfish ploy on my part. I've been wanting to get my hands on these Arabians since I first laid eyes on them."

"I see." Virginia plucked a strand of hay and broke it into four even pieces. It gave her something to do with

Indiscreet

her hands. Otherwise she might have had to sit on them in order to keep them to herself.

"I don't want you to misunderstand why I requested you," she said.

He cocked an eyebrow in her direction, but his hands never ceased their efficient movements. There was no sound in the stable except the soft scraping of the curry comb and the cooing of pigeons in the loft.

"It's not because of the way you look. I'm sure women have told you, you're gorgeous."

"Not lately." His smile was guileless. "In fact, not ever."

"They should have. By the droves."

"Do droves of men tell you how beautiful you are?"

"No. Not even one, unless you count Eldon Prescott at the post office."

"He must be a man of good taste."

Virginia cupped her knees and drew them up to her chest. The sun enhanced the bronze tones of Bolton's skin and gave his black hair the sheen of a raven's wing. Except for his blue eyes, he looked every inch the savage, as if he might leap onto the stallion's back at any moment and ride off with her captive. And she wouldn't even give a yelp of protest, not a single one.

Her friend Jane would laugh if she could hear Virginia describe the scene. "The thing I like about you, Virginia," she'd say, "is that you know how to turn drab reality into pulsating fantasy."

It would behoove Virginia to get her head out of the clouds and her feet back on the ground.

"Eldon Prescott's a man of indiscriminate taste," she

said. "He tells every woman in Pontotoc the same thing. 'Good morning, Miss Ruthie. My, aren't you beautiful today.' 'Hello, Lola Bell, what brings such a beautiful woman out on such a beautiful day?' "

"And are they?"

"Yes, if you look on the inside rather than the outside."

"I like him already, and I haven't even met him yet."

Virginia tensed. She was making a fool of herself, lolling around in the hay thinking she could have an ordinary conversation with a handsome man. The nature of her profession lifted her out of the ordinary, and Bolton Gray Wolf was not just any man. He was a journalist, that dread breed who probed her as coldly as a scientist then spread her secrets out for all the world to gossip about.

"Yet? Are you planning to ask Eldon Prescott what the real Virginia Haven is like?" She jumped off the bale of hay and dusted the seat of her jeans. "Let me save you the trouble. I'm tough and independent and rich—I'm very, very rich—but I'm not sneaky and I'm not mean. I don't lie and I don't pretend. So don't you ever pretend with me, Bolton Gray Wolf. Don't you ever pretend to be this charming friendly young man who adores horses when all you want to do is sneak off behind my back and start trying to dig up dirt on me."

"Have you finished?"

"Not quite. Don't think you can weasel your way into my good graces *or* my bed with all that Apache charm. I have no intention of being a conquest. Not yours, not anybody's."

Indiscreet

13

Bolton had never met a woman with such a sharp stinger. The problem was, he'd long ago ceased to think of Virginia Haven as an interview. When she'd sat on that bale of hay with the sun in her hair and on her fair skin, he'd thought of her as all woman, all *desirable* woman. As a matter of fact, he'd lost his professional detachment about the time she'd dismounted from the Arabian and stood in front of him with her hair whipping around her face. She reminded him of sunshine and roses. More than that she set off a fire in his blood, a fire of such proportions, he knew it wasn't a fluke, and that it wouldn't go away no matter what she said or did.

With her feet wide apart and her hands on her hips, she waited.

"Well, aren't you going to defend yourself?"

He smiled at her. "No."

"I suppose you're going to pack up your cameras and hightail it to the nearest airport."

"No." He draped blankets over the horses and led them to their stalls.

Some of the starch went out of Virginia. She'd never met a man she couldn't back down. And she'd certainly never met a journalist who didn't grovel at her feet for the sake of a story.

"What are you going to do?"

"Do you want me to answer that question, Virginia, or have you already decided what my answers will be?"

"Don't play word games with me. You'll lose."

"I never lose, Virginia."

His eyes cut through her like brilliant blue lasers. She felt exposed, as if he'd stripped away her skin and left nothing standing except bare bones and a heart, a heart beating too hard and too fast.

There was a slow and easy grace in the way he moved, as if the act of retrieving cameras and gear was some ancient, ritualistic dance. With any other man she'd have said his movements were carefully calculated, but Virginia was not dumb. If she'd learned anything in the last few minutes, it was that Bolton Gray Wolf was definitely not just *any* man.

The sun turned him to some kind of god as he stood facing her with cameras slung over his shoulders. She'd read about bones melting, but until that moment she'd never understood the concept. Feeling behind her with one hand, she slowly sank back onto the bale of hay.

"When you're ready for this interview, call me. I'm staying at the Ramada in Tupelo." He scrawled the number on the back of his business card and handed it to her. She refused to reach for the card, and he placed it on the hay. Though he never touched her, she could feel the heat of his hand as if he had slowly and deliberately caressed her hip.

She looked up at him and became trapped in his intense gaze.

"And Virginia . . . when I come to your bed, you won't be a conquest. You will be an equal."

He walked away with the same silent grace he'd used in rubbing down her horses. She wrapped her arms around herself and watched him go. She was still sitting that way when Candace came to the barn.

"What are you doing, Mother?"

How could she tell her daughter that she had no

earthly idea? That she'd been turned inside out and upside down ever since Bolton Gray Wolf had come on the scene?

"What are *you* doing, Candace?"

"I came to tell you that Jane called to remind you about dinner tonight . . . and to lead you to the house in case you'd forgotten the way."

Laughing, Virginia stood up and put her arm around her daughter's waist.

"Am I that bad?"

"Sometimes. But I've decided to keep you anyhow."

"Good, because I've decided to keep you too."

They started toward the house arm in arm, their heads close together as they talked.

"Did you finish the interview?"

"No."

"Mother! You didn't run this one off, did you?"

"No. He's not the kind of man who can be run off. Besides, these interviews take longer than one afternoon."

"How long?"

"A few days, I expect. Maybe even a week or longer."

"Good. Maybe he'll still be here when I come home next weekend. Marge will think he's a dreamboat." Candace glanced at her mother. "I thought I'd bring her home with me, if you don't mind."

"Of course not."

Marge's home was in Montana, and weekends on the college campus were very long for her. Sometimes Virginia felt as if she had two daughters instead of one, which was fine with her. In fact, better than fine. It was good to have young people around. It kept her from thinking too much about the severe limitations of her social life.

That evening over fried dill pickles at the Front Porch in nearby Tupelo, Jane reminded her.

"You need to get out more, Virginia."

"I *am* out."

"Oh, poop. Not with me. With somebody handsome, well hung, and loaded."

"Jane, a man would have to rob a Brink's truck to have more money than me, and I'm not interested in some brainless jock."

"You have not been interested in any man since Roger dumped you."

"That's not true." Virginia dragged the appetizers closer to her plate. "You're hogging all the dill pickles."

"You're changing the subject."

"I certainly am. I can think of nothing more boring than my social life."

"See. That's just what I told you. You spend too much time at your computer, Virginia. Computers can't hold you close at night, and they certainly can't give you orgasms."

"Jane, did I ever tell you that you have a one-track mind?"

"Yeah. Every day since we turned sixteen. If you weren't rich and famous, I'd hate you."

"And if you didn't have freckles and red hair, I'd hate

Indiscreet

you. It's hard to hate somebody who looks like Orphan Annie."

Laughing, Jane patted her pouf of red hair. "Do you think it looks natural? Lola tried a new color on me today. It's called siren-red."

"I like it, Jane. It'll stop traffic. As a matter of fact—" Virginia stopped in midsentence.

"Virginia . . . *Virginia*, what in the world are you staring at?"

When Virginia didn't respond, Jane turned toward the door.

"Holy Moses! Who is *that*?" Jane clutched the front of her dress in a pretended swoon. "I could eat him with a silver spoon. Heck, I could eat him with a tin spoon if he'd just come close enough. . . . Good Lord, he's coming this way." Jane grabbed her purse and hastily applied a fresh coat of lipstick. "Do I look all right? *Virginia* . . ."

In the few hours since she'd last seen him, Bolton Gray Wolf had lost none of his good looks. As a matter of fact, Virginia's memories hadn't done him justice. Quite simply, he took her breath away.

"Hello, Virginia."

"Bolton."

She gave him a curt nod and refused to yield to her urge to anchor herself to the table with a death grip. He'd swapped his denim shirt for a soft butternut leather, open at the neck to reveal a glimpse of dark hair.

"I didn't expect to see you this evening." He smiled as if he knew secrets. Lord, did he know hers?

"Even novelists have to eat."

18

"Virginia . . ." Jane said, then cleared her throat with a sound that was half lady, half pit bull. It was the signal she'd used with her best friend for years to let Virginia know that she was out of bounds, out of order, and threatening to be out of grace.

Virginia felt relief. And then hard on its heels, regret. For a moment she'd fancied herself all alone in the restaurant with Bolton.

She made the introductions smoothly then watched as he turned his charm toward her best friend. He didn't flirt but merely used that natural easy grace that probably came from living wild and free in the mountains of Arizona.

She knew about him, had made it a point of knowing about him. Not just about his work, which was superb, but about his history, his personal life. She'd worked too hard building her career and recreating her life to trust just anybody with something as important as an interview.

All the things she'd said to him at the stable aside, she knew Bolton Gray Wolf was not only brilliant, but honest and trustworthy. She also knew that he was intensely independent, working freelance, taking only the jobs that interested him. He preferred the company of horses and dogs to women, which probably accounted for the fact that he was still single. What amazed Virginia was that some cute young thing hadn't snatched him up long ago.

Maybe she ought to write every single female in the western half of the United States and thank them for leaving Bolton Gray Wolf to her. Or perhaps she ought

Indiscreet

to berate them for leaving so much temptation in her path.

He was still standing beside the table talking to Jane, but every now and then he sent Virginia one of those riveting looks that made her feel naked and exposed. God, he was dangerous.

Suddenly his full attention was on her. Bending over, he caught her hand.

"I'll expect to hear from you, Virginia . . . soon."

His touch, his look rendered her speechless. By the time she'd recovered, he had gone, vanished around the corner to one of the tables out of sight.

"Out of sight, out of mind," she muttered, knowing that she lied.

Leaning across the table, her face flushed and her eyes bright, Jane didn't even hear her. Which was just as well. Best to keep her feelings about Bolton to herself.

"Is he not the most gorgeous pulsating hunk of male pulchritude in the entire universe if not the whole solar system, or are they one and the same?" Jane fanned herself with her napkin. "Whew, I'm having a hot flash."

"You don't get hot flashes from viewing handsome men, and furthermore, it's a good thing you're a CPA instead of a writer. 'Pulsating hunk of male pulchritude,' is gross overstatement."

"What's got you so riled all of a sudden?" Jane squinted her eyes, then tossed her napkin to the center of the table and chortled with glee. "Well, well, well. Somebody of the male persuasion has finally gotten under your skin. Hoorah! Old Roger, move over."

"Bolton Gray Wolf is not under my skin. I barely know the man, for one thing."

"It only takes a moment," Jane said, quoting from a song they had both sung in the chorus of the community theater's spring production of *Hello, Dolly*.

"Plagiarism doesn't become you."

"He's awfully young, though." Jane picked up her menu and studied her friend over the top of it.

"Thirty-five, to be precise," Virginia said, and Jane arched her eyebrows. "You don't think I'd let him come near me without investigating him first, do you?"

"He's exactly what you need."

"Not *my needs* again."

Virginia threw up her hands, and Jane grinned.

"I feel reckless. I'm having fried catfish, fried hush puppies, and corn bread made with lots of grease." Jane shoved her menu aside. "I guess you're having broiled, as usual."

"Yes." Virginia's mind was not on food; it was on the man just around the corner, a man she couldn't even see.

"That's just what I mean. You need to take a chance, Virginia. Look, you've paid your dues. You don't have to be the independent woman showing everybody you can make it without Roger or his puny child support check. You've made it, kid, big time."

Jane waited until the waitress had taken their orders before she finished her diatribe.

"Everybody knows that women reach their sexual peak later than men. Take that gorgeous young hunk to bed, then send him on his merry way. Both of you will still be grinning come Christmas."

Indiscreet

The trouble was, if she ever took him to bed, she wouldn't want to let him go. Virginia understood that on some deep primeval level. But it was not information that she cared to share, even with her nearest and dearest friend.

Virginia shoved the appetizer plate toward her friend.

"Eat your dill pickles and shut up."

"You wouldn't like me if I did. You'd be bored."

Jane was right, of course. Virginia thrived on challenge, and she adored going against convention. But wouldn't it be lovely sometime to sit back and let somebody else fight the battles, to lie on Egyptian cotton sheets and let somebody kiss away her worries and soothe away her aches?

Not just somebody. Bolton Gray Wolf.

He couldn't get her off his mind, not even when he saw her empty table. As he walked through the restaurant, Bolton studied every nook and cranny, looked twice at every woman with honey-blond hair, hoping for a glimpse of Virginia.

She stayed with him on the drive back to his motel and all the while he surfed through the channels. He was not one to watch television, but, cooped up in his room, there was nothing else to do. Each image on the screen brought to mind some small detail of Virginia. The female reporter on the ten o'clock news had lips nearly as ripe and rosy as hers. The first guest on the late show had her long, slender legs; the next, her throaty chuckle.

He closed his eyes and saw Virginia galloping across the fields on her white Arabian, saw the autumn leaves and dust swirling around her so that she approached him like someone in a dream, half hidden by soft golden mists. He yearned to tear aside the veil of mystery that shrouded her, to discover all her desires, all her secrets.

When the late show was over, he began to undress for bed. The ring box fell out of his pocket. Guilty, he picked it up. He had promised to call Janice when he got to Mississippi.

He glanced at the clock, hoping it was too late. Almost midnight. He could tell himself that she'd already be asleep, that there was no need to wake her, but he'd never been one to lie, not even to himself. Janice would be waiting up for him, anxious, maybe even crying.

He picked up the phone, and she answered on the first ring.

"Bolton. Where in the world are you?"

"Northeast Mississippi, home of Elvis Presley and Virginia Haven."

"That woman you've gone to interview."

"Yes, that woman."

He could hear her soft sniffle, then the forced cheer in her voice.

"I don't want you to think I've been hanging around the phone waiting, Bolton. I know you're perfectly capable of taking care of yourself. I'm not the least bit worried."

"That's great, Janice."

"Bolton . . ." Again that small sniffle. "I don't have anything to worry about, do I?"

Indiscreet

23

He fingered the ring box he'd laid on the bedside table.

"Not a thing, Janice."

Except a woman called Virginia Haven, a woman who had galloped her white Arabian through the golden leaves of autumn and straight into his heart.

THREE

The first thing Virginia did when she woke up was reach for the phone. She'd call Bolton to do the interview and get it over with. Then he could go back to Apache land and she could go back to her safe and trusty computer.

As she reached for the receiver she caught sight of her face in the three-way mirror over her dressing table. Without a speck of makeup she looked every bit of forty-eight, if not more. She'd bathe and repair the damage and *then* she'd call Bolton.

She'd been in one of her reckless moods when she designed her bathroom. It had floor-to-ceiling windows that faced a private courtyard and skylights that she could open in summertime to let the morning sun pour down on banks of ferns. Virginia could never get enough light in her house. As if all that natural light weren't enough, one full wall of mirrors was surrounded by incandescent bulbs.

It was a bathroom made for lovers, with space for

tumbling naked on the floor together, a tub big enough for frolic, and plenty of mirrors to view the fun.

As she leaned over the tub and turned on the water, Virginia thought again of Bolton.

"When I come to your bed, you won't be a conquest. You will be an equal." Her mind replayed Bolton's soft, seductive promise. Not *if*, but *when*.

She closed her eyes and imagined being in his bed, in his arms. A small groan escaped her, and then another. Desire long repressed came boiling to the surface. Passion long held at bay swept through her. With her gift for fantasy, she imagined a Bolton so real that she reached out and caressed his fine, hard body with her left hand. With her other she brought herself to a trembling climax.

The sound of cascading water drew her back to reality. Her bath was threatening to overflow and flood her floor. Sunlight, relentless and unmerciful, poured through the windows and illuminated a middle-aged woman with cellulite and a belly that would never be flat again.

She'd always been one of those people who blithely said that age was all in the mind, but today she felt the mantle of her years. Today she wished for a windowless bathroom. Today she wished for dark clouds over the sun and shades drawn over all the windows.

What could Bolton possibly see in a woman her age?

Virginia climbed quickly into the tub so she could shut out the view of all the damage done by years of wear and tear, by an appendectomy and a hysterectomy, by giving birth and giving too much of herself to her career, by anxiety about the past and worry over the future.

What kind of fool was she, anyhow? Dreaming of a man thirteen years her junior?

Angry, she sloshed water haphazardly over herself, then stalked to her bedroom, dripping all over the floor. She found Bolton's card on the antique table beside her bed.

"Be there," she said to herself as she dialed.

"Bolton Gray Wolf."

She was held momentarily speechless by the sound of his voice.

"Dammit," she whispered.

"I beg your pardon? Virginia?"

"I dropped the phone."

"I see."

There was laughter in his voice. Was he laughing at her?

"Be here in one hour sharp," she snapped. "Let's get this interview over with."

"I'll be there."

"I'll be ready."

"Good."

There was laughter in his voice again. Ready? Lord, was she ever *ready* . . . A hot flush came over her as she remembered what she'd done in the bathroom. She hung up without saying good-bye, then sat heavily on the edge of her bed and stared at the telephone.

"Mother?" Candace poked her head around the bedroom door. "Aren't you coming down to breakfast? I'm leaving in half an hour to go back to school."

Indiscreet

"Sorry, honey. I forgot."

How could she forget something as important to Candace as the Sigma Chi fraternity dance? Virginia threw on her pink terry cloth robe and raked a brush through her hair.

"You look gorgeous, sweetheart." She put her arm around her daughter's waist and together they went down the stairs to the breakfast room. "You're going to knock Walford's eyes out."

"Wexford."

"Wexford. Beaufort, is it?"

"Yeah. From Shreveport. Every woman on campus is going to be pea-green with envy." Candace cast a disapproving eye on Virginia's plate.

"Mother, is that all you're eating?"

"Fruit and cereal. It's a perfect breakfast."

"Four little sections of grapefruit and half a cup of cereal? Yeah. Perfect, if you're a bird."

"When you get to be my age, honey, you have to count fat grams."

Candace's laughter was affectionate. "How many more years do you think I have to eat banana splits with mountains of whipped cream and popcorn dripping with real butter?"

"Plenty. Make the most of them, honey."

"I plan to." Candace stood up and kissed Virginia on the cheek. "I've had a good example to follow."

Virginia escorted her daughter to the car, then stood in the driveway waving as the sky-blue Thunderbird convertible disappeared down the winding driveway.

As she watched, another car came up the driveway, a

red Mustang with Bolton Gray Wolf at the wheel. How appropriate that even the car he rented was named after a horse, she thought.

"I'm early," he said. He looked fresh and delicious standing in the morning sunlight with his cameras slung over his shoulders, his face just shaved, and his hair untamed. She could imagine how he had looked standing in front of the small bathroom mirror in his motel room, trying to subdue that mane of wild black hair.

She wished she'd been there to help him. The thought made her smile.

Bolton aimed, and the shutter clicked.

"I look awful." Virginia held a hand over her face.

"Don't." Gently Bolton moved her hand, then tipped her face upward. Her breath caught in her throat. Something magical bloomed between them, and for a moment she thought he was going to kiss her. She *wanted* him to kiss her.

"You're soft and beautiful in the morning sun." He stepped backward, his camera clicking and whirring. "Pink becomes you."

His voice mesmerized her. She *felt* soft and beautiful. Even without her makeup. Even with her hair not fixed. Even with her crow's-feet showing in the sun.

"You have a lovely smile, Virginia."

"Thank you." He was enough to make an Egyptian mummy smile. "I didn't expect you this soon. Did you mean to catch me off guard?"

He took one more shot, then changed film in his camera. When he had finished, he slung the camera over his shoulder, stepped in close, and gazed down at her.

Indiscreet

"No, Virginia. An hour was too long to wait to see you."

The heat started in her cheeks, spread over her neck, and across her breasts. He was dangerous and persuasive. And she was alone with him, alone with nothing on under her robe. Reason told her to back him off, to put him in his place. Her heart told her otherwise.

"Why?" she said.

"For this." He cupped her face and drew her gently to him. There was no hurry in him, no urgency, just a beautiful certainty as he fitted their bodies together, legs touching, hips perfectly matched, chests pressed close. He draped her arms around his neck and wrapped his around her waist and back.

His embrace felt so good, so damned good.

"And this," he whispered. Then he took her lips. It was not an assault but a kiss as soft as the first rains of summer.

Virginia didn't stop to weigh consequences; she just let go.

His lips were tender, his breath sweet, and his kiss as whisper soft as the brush of butterfly wings against rose petals.

"Virginia . . ." he whispered.

"Bolton . . . we shouldn't."

"We've already gone beyond that. It's fate. Out of our control."

She took his hand and led him into her house. He needed no urging. At the foot of the staircase he swept her into his arms and carried her up.

"To the left," she whispered.

There was no pausing at the bedroom door. Boldly he carried her inside. In a slow, sensuous movement he let her slide down his body until her feet touched the floor.

He dropped his cameras onto the chaise longue, his shirt on the dressing stool, and his pants and shoes beside the bed.

Naked, he was a work of art. Without speaking, she walked around him, touching, letting her fingers graze the magnificent breadth of his chest, sinking them into the fine dark hair, running them down his belly and over his erection.

He smiled at her, a secret smile that held promises, promises too delicious to postpone. Silently he lifted her into his arms and spread her across the bed. Kneeling over her, he traced her cheekbones, her brow, her lips with his fingertips. A lock of black hair hung over his forehead, and she gently brushed it back.

"I want to see your face," she said, letting her fingers memorize him. "You take my breath away."

Slowly he untied her sash, peeled off her robe, and flung it onto the floor.

"You won't be needing that."

When he entered her she thought she had died and gone to heaven. She was so wet for him, so wet and so very hungry.

"Love me, Bolton." She wrapped her arms tightly around him and drew him close. "Love me."

"I am. I'm loving you, Virginia."

His rhythms were as graceful as music, and the song invaded every part of Virginia, its cadences and harmonies balm for her body, her heart, her soul. She felt reborn, as if the woman who had struggled to prove herself over and over again had vanished and in her place was somebody with wings, somebody who knew how to fly.

"You are so good," she murmured, "so very, very good."

"*We're* good. It's us, Virginia, you and me together."

Buried deep inside her, he paused and studied her face. His sudden smile was as dazzling as the sun.

"I've spent all my life looking for you."

"Shhh." She put her hand over his lips. "Don't say things in the heat of passion that you won't mean in the cold light of day."

"I never say things I don't mean." He took up his rhythm again. "*Never.*"

There was none of the awkwardness of new lovers between them. Their minds were as connected as their bodies. A mere thought from her became action from him. He understood her sighs, her moans, her screams of ecstasy. He knew her moods, her desires, her preferences.

She peaked again and again, and still Bolton loved her. With an endurance born of youth and a strength born of training, he satisfied her in a way no man ever had, in a way no man ever would.

The years rolled away, the years of sacrificing her own desires for the sake of her child and her career, and she was once again a woman, a woman by turns tender and bawdy, gentle and fiery. She felt fulfillment and hunger at the same time. It was her hunger that made her grip him hard around his waist and hold him tight.

"Don't leave," she said fiercely. "Don't you dare leave."

"This is where I belong, Virginia. With you, like this, buried deep inside you, satisfying you, satisfying me."

When he smiled, his eyes lit from inside, and as she gazed into that blue fire she knew that the impossible had happened. Bolton Gray Wolf filled more than her body; he filled her heart. What they had between them was not sex; it was love. Mere sex wouldn't make her feel as if she'd reached up and touched stars. Mere sex wouldn't make her feel as if her soul had separated from her body and joined his, as if her very body had cast aside its wrappings and somehow become one with his.

She longed to cry out her newly discovered truth. She longed to cup his face and look deep into his eyes and say, "I love you." Already she was certain of heartbreak. To tell that secret would ensure disaster. For both of them.

Tears stung her eyes and slid down her cheeks.

"Virginia?" He touched a single teardrop, softly, tenderly. "Why are you crying?"

"Because this is so wonderful, and I am so hungry. So very hungry for you."

"You don't have to be hungry, ever again."

She believed him. For the beautiful moments they lay together in her bed she believed that all she had to do was reach out and Bolton would be there, all she had to do was call and he would come running, all she had to do was wish for this magical joining and he would make it happen.

But when the loving was over, when they lay tangled together on her sheets, sweating and sated, she knew that she was being the worst kind of fool, the kind who believed in miracles. She'd learned long ago that the only miracles were those earned by sweat and toil and intelligence and perseverance and sacrifice.

Bolton laced their fingers together and squeezed.

"I love you, Virginia."

She squeezed her eyes against the quick tears that threatened to shame her and embarrass them both.

"Don't," she said. "You don't have to say things like that. I'm a big girl. I can take the truth."

"What is the truth?"

"I needed this but now it's over and done with and neither of us has to pretend it was anything except great sex."

"That's not the truth, Virginia."

She pulled away from him, put on her robe, and curled up on the chaise longue.

"I've been called worse names than a liar." She folded her hands tightly together to keep them from betraying her with their awful shaking.

Without a word Bolton got off the bed, knelt beside the chaise, and gently unfolded her hands. Then he kissed her fingertips, one by one. His actions were far more revealing than denials.

"If what we had was just good sex, why are you trembling?"

"I didn't get enough sleep last night. I'm an insomniac. It happens with age."

He said nothing, merely lifted one caustic eyebrow.

She stared at him, waiting for him to fill the silence with excuses, waiting for him to push her into anger. She *was* mad, damned mad, and she wanted some reason to show it. Tilting her chin up, she dared him to give her a reason.

Bolton remained as implacable as the mountain from which he had come. Still kneeling, he began a slow, erotic massage of her feet. That alone was enough to make Virginia forget her anger and confusion, make her forget that he might be after her money or her secrets or both, make her forget the horrible age gap that separated them. When his hands moved over her legs, she knew she was lost and nothing else mattered except his touch.

Closing her eyes, she let herself go limp. Bolton Gray Wolf was mesmerizing, and he worked a slow, seductive magic on her.

"That feels so good," she whispered.

"Yes, it does."

He untied the sash and opened her robe so that she lay upon the chaise like a fallen flower. He tasted her, lingering so long that she lost all reason. When she had climaxed and lay limp, he lifted her into his arms and held her tightly against his chest.

"This is not about your money," he said, as if he had read her mind. "It's not about your profession and mine. It's about us, Virginia. It's about love."

She was too far gone to argue with him. She was burning, burning, and only he knew how to handle her fire. She laced her arms tightly around his neck and laid her head on his chest.

Indiscreet

"Take me back to bed, Bolton."

"And then what, Virginia?"

"You know. . . ."

"Say it."

"Are you going to make me beg?"

"No. I want to hear you say the words." His eyes were so intensely blue, she was almost blinded by them. "Say the words, Virginia."

"They're just words."

"Say them."

She closed her eyes, but even then she could see his face, naked with emotion.

"They're just words," she repeated, closing her eyes to shut out his face. His lips brushed hers softly, tenderly. And she was lost.

"Make love to me," she whispered.

"Yes. I will love you."

He lowered her to the bed and slid inside her. Pinioned against the sheets, she looked up at him. There was no triumph in his face, no sense of victory, only love, raw and pure.

"And you will love me." It was the last thing he said to her, the last thing that needed to be said.

What they did in her bedroom needed no words. What they did was too beautiful for words, too powerful, too sacred. What happened between them was a rare gift, too precious to cast aside.

Virginia held that gift close to her heart. She knew that it wouldn't last forever. She knew that as soon as his job was finished he would leave her bed and never look back, leave Mississippi and forget about the woman whose heart he had stolen.

One week. Two. It didn't matter how long he stayed. What mattered was what they did with the time. Call her selfish, call her foolish, call her anything at all, but Virginia knew what she was, understood what she was doing.

She was a woman who had spent too many years in the twin prisons of responsibility and fame. Bolton had handed her the key, and she was going to take it. For today and tomorrow and all the days that he was in Mississippi, she was going to be free. And when he was gone she'd shut herself up with her responsibilities and her computer and her money and her fame and never look back with regret.

Never.

FOUR

He photographed her leaning against an oak tree with the late-afternoon sun filtering through the leaves and dappling her with gold.

"You are so beautiful," he said. "Soft and lush and satisfied."

"You make me feel that way."

He took aim, and she tilted her head back, laughing. He captured her that way, happier than she ever remembered being, in love with him, in love with life, in love with the world. A shower of leaves fell on her white blouse and settled in the folds of her full peasant skirt. She bent over to brush them away, then changed her mind and playfully flicked them in his direction. With cameras whirring, he caught her in the falling leaves, caught her as she moved in close, eyes gleaming with erotic intent.

Camera forgotten, they tumbled among the leaves as playful as children. Their playfulness quickly turned to passion, and they made slow, beautiful love on a golden carpet of leaves with the sun burnishing their skin.

"I can't get enough of you," she said.

"You don't have to get enough of me, Virginia. I'm here. I'll be here."

Almost, she could believe it was true. Full of him, full of pleasure, full of joy, she could imagine herself waking every day to find Bolton beside her, reaching out to touch the pillow that had been empty for so many years and finding this magnificent man who could turn her inside out with a single glance.

Propped on her elbows, she gazed down at him.

"Are you hungry?" she asked.

"For food or you?"

"Food. We missed lunch, and if we keep this up, we're going to miss dinner."

"It's a sacrifice I'm willing to make."

"Me too." She kissed him lightly on the cheek, then stood up and adjusted her clothes. "However, if you're to keep up your strength, you have to eat."

She loved his hearty masculine laughter, loved the way he lifted her off the ground and hugged her close. Noses touching, lips a hairbreadth away, he whispered, "You want me to keep up my strength, do you?"

"Yes."

"Any reason I should know about?"

"If you're as smart as I think you are, you probably already know the reason."

"Indulge me. Tell me."

"For this." She kissed him, lightly at first and then with such intensity that they were both left breathless.

"And this." She ran her tongue down the side of his neck. "And this." She caressed his back, as far down as her arms would reach.

"That will do for starters." He nudged open the front of her blouse and took her nipple deep into his mouth.

Goose bumps the size of golf balls ran over her.

"You like that, don't you, Virginia?"

"Yes. I like everything you do to me."

"Not *to* you. With you. Love has to be reciprocal."

There it was again. *Love.*

"Why do you insist on using that word, Bolton?"

"Because it's true."

She tried to wiggle her way out of his arms, but he wouldn't let her go.

"Put me down, Bolton."

"Why? So you can huff off somewhere and try to justify your mistaken notions?"

"*I* don't have any mistaken notions. I know exactly what this is: It's a wildly passionate affair that will end as soon as this interview is over."

"I'm not doing the interview."

"What?"

"You heard me. I won't do the interview."

"But you *have* to. It's your job."

"I choose the jobs I want to do. I'm choosing not to do this one."

He set her on her feet and pinned her against the tree.

"You can't do that," she said.

"Do what, Virginia? Keep you pinned against this

tree?" His eyes sparkled with mischief as he pressed his hips closer. "Just watch me."

"You're impossible."

"I'm half Apache. We're known for taking the women we love captive, especially ornery, opinionated, stubborn women like you."

"Stubborn? I don't hold a candle to you, Bolton Gray Wolf."

"What happened to make you so distrustful of men, Virginia?"

"Is this an interview question?"

"I told you, I'm no longer doing the interview."

"Dammit, Bolton. You *have* to."

"Why?"

"Because I've promised to grant one interview, and if you don't do it, then I'll be stuck with some arrogant upstart who'd like nothing better than to dish the dirt on me."

"Does that mean you no longer suspect me of going to bed with you so I can learn your secrets?"

"I didn't say that."

"Not exactly in those words."

"Look . . . can I help it if I have this built-in distrust of journalists?"

"Haven't we gone beyond that, Virginia? When are you going to start viewing me as a person instead of a profession? When are you going to learn to trust me?"

"You're tough. No wonder you're good."

"In bed or in the magazines?"

"Both," she said. Bolton's smile was slow and easy.

Indiscreet

"All right . . . all right. I admit it. I trust you, Bolton. As much as I can trust any of you."

"Good. Then I'll do the interview."

He studied her for so long, she felt as if he were probing her with laser beams.

"Back to my original question: What happened to make you distrust men?"

This time he didn't protest when she walked away. With the instinct given to all men who love nature, he understood that there were times when all creatures must be free. He knew that unless he let Virginia go, he could never keep her, never even *hope* to keep her.

Her stride was long and determined, and for a moment it looked as if she meant to stalk all the way to her house and never look back. He stood with his feet firmly planted, resisting the urge to follow her.

There was something magnificent in her anger. The way her skirts swished left no doubt in his mind that underneath was a body seething and ready to explode. That was one of the things he loved about Virginia: She never did anything halfway. Whether she was making love or expressing her rage, she put her entire self into it. With her there was no pouting, no retreating into silence. With Virginia, he knew exactly where he stood.

And at the moment, he was at the edge of the woods all by himself, literally as well as figuratively.

He knew the minute she made up her mind to turn back. Her skirt told the story. The angry, swishing skirt began a gentle swaying. Bolton held his breath, watching. The sun had all but disappeared, leaving a red-gold glow that reflected in Virginia's honey-colored hair and on her fair skin.

It was a picture too good to miss. He aimed and fired. He would never tire of watching Virginia, never tire of photographing her. With or without the lens she was a subject worthy of hours and days and years of contemplation.

When she turned and saw the camera, she smiled.

"You can't resist a good shot, can you?" she said.

"I can't resist you."

She came back up the path to him, and he didn't stop shooting until she stood two feet away, eyes lifted to his.

"You are irresistible," she whispered. "I can't walk away from you like that."

He took her hands, lifted them to his lips, and kissed her open palms.

"Virginia, you don't have to tell me anything you don't want to. Your past doesn't matter to me. All that matters is us . . . here . . . now."

"No, I need to tell you . . ." She withdrew her hands and stepped back as if touching him while she talked might taint him. "It was a long time ago . . . I was younger then, naive in many ways, especially about men. Roger was the only man I'd ever known . . . intimately."

The confession made her self-conscious, and she turned her face from him. He caressed her cheek lightly, once, making no attempt to turn her face back to his.

That one touch was enough. Virginia faced him once more.

Indiscreet

"I guess that makes me hopelessly outdated," she said.

"It makes you hopelessly wonderful."

"Don't," she whispered. Quickly she shut her eyes so she wouldn't see the love light shining in his. She'd seen that love light once, had thought it would burn forever. There was no such thing as forever. At least, not for Virginia Haven. Not with Roger, and certainly not with Bolton Gray Wolf.

What had gotten into her anyway? Baring her soul to him? Women bent on casual affairs didn't bare their souls.

Shrugging her shoulders, she attempted a light laugh.

"Look," she said. "It was nothing. He left me for another woman. Men do it every day."

Bolton was as still as the oak tree that stood sentry behind him. In the fading light she tried to study his face, but it was hidden in purple shadows. Why was he so still? Why didn't he say something?

She clenched her hands together, then hid them in the folds of her full skirt. Still, Bolton was silent.

"All right," she said. "He didn't just leave me for some stranger. Besides Jane, she was my best friend. Jane, Sandra, and Virginia, the Three Musketeers, one for all and all for one. I was teaching history, saving every penny I made so Roger and I could build our dream house. He not only took my best friend, he took all my money as well. It wasn't much, but it was all I had. If it hadn't been for Jane, Candace and I would not have had a place to stay."

"Jane's a lovely woman, Virginia."

"Yes, she is, inside and out."

"I don't want Jane. I want you." Bolton glanced over her vast estate. "This is an impressive place, but I prefer a simpler setting, mountains instead of tennis courts, woods instead of swimming pools, birch logs instead of brick and stone." He took both her hands. When she tried to jerk away, he held on tightly. "I don't want your money, Virginia. If you gave every penny of it away, I'd still be in love with you."

Cursing the darkness that hid her face from him, he waited for his words to sink in. He could tell by the stiffness of her body that she was still unconvinced. What would it take to make this woman believe how he loved her? What would he have to do to show her that the fire and magic between them was a once-in-a-lifetime thing?

"You push too hard, Bolton," his mother was always telling him. "Ever since you were born you've tried to control everything in your path. Sometimes you have to let go. Sometimes you have to let things happen."

He would give everything he owned, including his beloved horse and dog, if he could know the right thing to say, the right thing to do so that Virginia would let down her guard and let him love her. But when it came to matters of the heart, he was a novice. And so he decided to simply let things happen.

Gathering her into his arms, he held her close. Her rigid stance told him that she was merely allowing this embrace, and perhaps only for the moment.

"It's all right, Virginia," he whispered, pressing his

cheek against her hair. The silky strands were as soft as a sigh against his skin. "We won't speak of these things."

Relief flooded through her. She stood on tiptoe and kissed his cheek.

"Let's go inside and raid the refrigerator," she said.

"Let's go."

Linking hands, they raced down the path together. Then together they created a feast as unconventional as it was huge, scrambled eggs and pasta salad, graham crackers with melted marshmallows and chocolate on top, iced tea with a sprig of mint, and toast cut in the shape of hearts. Bolton did the cutting, and she did the supervising. The result was eight perfect hearts spread with butter and raspberry jam.

"Too pretty to eat," she said.

"Unless you're starving." He ate two at one time. "I'm glad I thought of them."

"Hey, the hearts were my idea."

"I beg your pardon. That's outright plagiarism."

"Guilty." She held out her hands, laughing. "Take me captive. Punish me."

He carried her up the stairs, and they made slow, exquisite love while the moon made changing patterns across the sheets.

"I wish you had brought your clothes so you could stay the night," she said.

"I don't need anything except you, Virginia." He yawned and stretched flat on his back. "I'll get my clothes in the morning."

It was that simple. Bolton was moving in with her. At least until Candace came home.

Virginia wasn't going to think about that. Not yet. What she'd think about was the glorious week ahead.

Bolton was already asleep. Spread across her sheets gloriously naked, his right hand resting on her stomach and his left flung above his head, he took up most of her bed. Smiling, Virginia curled next to him. She loved the smell of him, the feel of him, the look of him.

The last thing she thought about before she fell asleep was that when she woke up in the morning, Bolton would be there.

He kissed her awake. His kisses were sweet and damp, falling on her cheek, her ear, her nose, her lips. When she opened her eyes she was dazzled by the sight of him bending over her naked.

"Good morning," he said.

Automatically she started reaching for her robe. Morning meant another day to write, another day to prove herself.

"What time is it?" she asked.

"Early." He eased her back to the bed and tucked the covers under her chin. "Don't get up. I wanted to let you know that I'm going to take a quick shower, then run back to the motel and get my things."

"Hmmm." She snuggled under the covers. "Okay."

Somewhere in the back of her mind was the idea of joining him in the shower, then putting on jogging pants and racing toward the barn and saddling the horses. Oh, there was so much they could do together, so much she could show him.

Indiscreet

The next thing she knew the doorbell was ringing. She grabbed her robe.

"Bolton?" she called, but all she heard was the sound of the shower. The doorbell pinged again. "Coming," she yelled, racing down the stairs.

Jane stood on her front porch, dressed in hot-pink sweats that clashed with her hair.

"Jane . . ." Flustered, Virginia cinched her belt tighter and smoothed her hair. "What in the world?"

"You told me to come over here for a morning jog come hell or high water. Of course, you forgot to mention that you'd be otherwise engaged." Jane plucked an oak leaf out of Virginia's hair. "I hope the Apache was as good in the sack as he looked like he'd be."

"Shhh, he might hear you."

"That is his car in the driveway, isn't it?"

"Yes."

"Where is he?"

"Upstairs . . . in the shower."

"Aha! This is getting better and better." Jane punched her friend's arm. "Good for you, old gal."

Virginia grabbed Jane and dragged her into the kitchen where the danger of being overheard was lessened.

"My Lord." Hands on hips, Jane surveyed the kitchen. "What happened in here? An orgy, I hope."

Virginia felt her face flush.

"We didn't clean up after dinner."

"Dinner?" Inspecting pots, pans, and plates, Jane popped a leftover graham cracker treat into her mouth. "It looks like breakfast, lunch, *and* dinner, to me. I hope that means you were too busy with more exciting things to eat."

"None of your business."

"Hey, I'm the one who told you to have at it. Remember?"

As much as Virginia loved Jane, she felt a disloyalty to Bolton in letting her best friend describe what they had done as "having at it."

"It wasn't like that, Jane."

Something in the quiet conviction of Virginia's tone made Jane wary. She turned her inspection on Virginia.

"Hey, now. . . . My Lord!" Jane sat down heavily at the table. "I need something to drink."

Virginia got two cups from the cupboard.

"Hot tea or coffee?"

"I don't care as long as it's laced with plenty of sugar."

The old friends were silent as Virginia heated water, measured instant coffee, then added cream and a heaping portion of sugar to Jane's cup. Completely at ease now, Virginia leaned back in her chair and enjoyed her morning coffee.

"I've never seen you so . . . *glowy*," Jane said.

"I feel good. Better than good. *Wonderful.*"

Jane plopped her cup in its saucer so hard, it rattled. Leaning across the table, she grabbed Virginia's hands and squeezed.

"Now you listen to me, Virginia. Don't you *dare* fantasize about this. Don't you dare tell me you've fallen in love."

"All right. I won't."

Indiscreet

49

From upstairs came the sound of Bolton's footsteps as he moved around the bedroom, dressing. A feeling as lovely as roses blooming overcame Virginia. Glancing through the open doorway and in the direction of the stairs, she gave a small secret smile.

"*Virginia . . .*"

"I'm not going to do anything foolish, Jane."

"Why am I not convinced? Is it because you've taken to going to bed with oak leaves in your hair? Or is it those hickeys all over your neck?"

Virginia drew the neck of her robe higher.

"Remember what happened with Harold," Jane said.

"That was six years ago."

"You thought he was the next best thing to sliced bread."

"He didn't fool me for long."

"He practically had you at the altar before you discovered he was planning to pay off all his gambling debts with your money and then retire and spend the rest of your money traveling over Europe."

"All right. So I made a mistake. But I'm not altar bound with Bolton Gray Wolf. I have better sense than that." A heavy silence fell over them as Jane studied her. "I don't want to hear it, Jane."

"What? I didn't say anything."

"Good. Don't."

They heard the sound of whistling, then footsteps on the stairs. Virginia smiled as if Christmas were coming and she was being granted a private audience with Santa.

"I guess this means the jog is off," Jane said.

"We'll jog, Jane . . . after Bolton has gone back to Arizona."

"I'm going to hold you to that, Virginia."

Virginia barely heard her, for Bolton Gray Wolf filled the doorway, and nothing else mattered.

FIVE

"Hi, Bolton, bye, Bolton. Gotta go," Jane said, but neither of them heard her.

Bolton leaned in the doorway drinking in the sight of Virginia, and she sat in her chair devouring him with her eyes. The chemistry between them was so sizzling that the air felt charged.

"You look delicious," Virginia said. "Good enough to eat."

"I was thinking the same thing about you."

Coming from any other man, the compliment would have sounded like flattery, but Virginia had learned that Bolton said what he meant and meant what he said, even when he was professing his love. There was no doubt in her mind that Bolton Gray Wolf loved her, but would he love her when he was forty and still turning heads and she was fifty-three and nothing was turning except her hair?

"Not only thinking, but *planning* . . ." he said, stalking her with passionate intent gleaming in his eyes.

He peeled off her robe and took her on the kitchen table, took her with such thoroughness that she was mindless with joy.

Time and again he brought her spiraling out of control, and when she finally protested that she didn't have an ounce of passion left, he proved her wrong. They shouted their completion at the same time, Virginia with a soft primal scream and Bolton in the beautiful musical language of his people.

"My Apache warrior," Virginia whispered, pulling him close, not wanting to let go, not now, not ever. "My magnificent, glorious, beautiful, lusty Apache warrior."

"I would fight ten thousand battles for you, Virginia. And win every one of them."

"You don't have to fight for me. I'm yours . . ." His eyes glowed with such triumph that she knew he'd misunderstood. ". . . for the rest of this week, at least."

For a moment it looked as if Bolton would protest. Instead she felt him grow hard again, and when he took her again, it was with such fierceness that she could think of nothing but him, see nothing but him, do nothing but scream out her pleasure, calling his name, over and over again.

When it was over, she rearranged her robe. Her hands shook as she reached for her coffee cup. Kneeling beside her, he caught her hands and brought them to his lips.

"I love you, Virginia. Now and always."

"Don't . . ." She batted her eyes against quick tears.

Indiscreet

"Don't spoil what we have." She cupped his face, not tenderly but urgently. "We have so little time. Every minute is precious. Please don't spoil this week with talk of the future."

"It's foolish to run from fate, Virginia. Sooner or later you're going to have to stop and face the truth. We belong together. Our futures are intertwined."

"We have no future, Bolton. End of discussion."

She jumped up and started cleaning the kitchen. Though she had a cleaning service three times a week, it gave her something to do, some reason to turn her back on the man who could seduce her with a single glance and steal her reason with a single smile.

He was so quiet that for a while she thought he'd gone. Then she felt his hands on her shoulders and his chest pressed against her back.

"All right, Virginia. End of discussion. At least for a while."

She understood that he was offering a compromise. She could either take it or face the alternative: Send him away and end it right there. She didn't know if she was too selfish, too hungry, too cowardly, or all three. All she knew was that as long as he was in Mississippi, she had to have Bolton Gray Wolf.

She patted his left hand. "You said something about going back to Tupelo to get your things."

"Yes." He turned her around and tipped her face up. "I'll be back, Virginia."

She smiled. "I never doubted for a minute that you would."

"Good. I don't want you to have any doubts about me."

His tone was serious again, and she wasn't about to tread into those deep waters. If she kept plunging in, she was liable to drown.

"Shoo." She grabbed a dish towel and playfully swatted his legs. "Scat. If you don't leave, I'm never going to get these oak leaves washed out of my hair."

As soon as he was out the door, she called and canceled all appointments for the week.

Leaving Virginia was hard, even for the short while it took to drive back to Tupelo, get the rest of his gear, and take care of his motel bill. But Bolton had to go. There was something more important than his motel bill that needed taking care of.

He dialed Janice's home number, thankful it was Sunday and he wouldn't have to say the things that needed to be said while she was at school. Her phone rang five times, and he had almost given up when she answered.

"Bolton? How wonderful to hear from you."

Janice's voice was full of expectations, and Bolton felt awash with sadness. What he had to say would hurt her, and he would never intentionally hurt a flea.

"How are you, Janice?"

"Great. I was outside gathering acorns and fall leaves for a little project at school. We're going to have an autumn festival, you see . . ."

When Janice got wound up about her children, the

Indiscreet

name she used to refer to her students, she could go on for hours. Bolton was not only patient with her stories, but interested in them. Janice was one of the unsung heroes who brought enthusiasm as well as skill and talent to the classroom, one of the thousands of great teachers whose only reward would be the success of the young people she taught. He admired her for what she did and loved her for the way she did it, loved her not as he loved Virginia, not in the soul-deep way of two people who were destined by fate to be together, but in the sweet, quiet way of friends who want only the best for each other.

Janice was breathless when she finished her tale.

"Oh, my. Just listen to me prattling on. How about you, Bolton. How is your trip?"

It was the perfect opening. He sent a quick prayer winging upward that he could tell the truth in the kindest way possible.

"Janice, sometimes things start out to be one thing and turn into another. That's what has happened to me. What started out to be an assignment turned out to be a miracle."

There was a small strangled cry on the other end of the line. If he could have done this any other way, he would have. He would have preferred being face-to-face with Janice, being there to hold her hand and wipe her tears, for he knew they were inevitable. But he couldn't live a lie. He couldn't be with Virginia while Janice was back home in Arizona thinking that he would come home to her.

There had to be an ending before he could hope for a beginning.

"What are you saying, Bolton?"

"Janice, you know that I think you're a wonderful woman—kind, sweet, talented, intelligent. You're a good friend and a good companion, and I enjoy your company. But I've never pretended to be in love with you."

"You've met someone else." Her calm manner surprised and pleased him. He'd been prepared to deal with hysterics.

"Yes, she's . . ."

"Bolton, listen to me. I don't care if you have a fling. Sometimes people get carried away . . ."

He could hear her mounting hysteria, and he wanted to stop her before she said things she'd later regret.

"Janice . . ."

". . . and then when they get back home they realize that nothing has changed, that they were just sowing a few wild oats . . . and that's okay with me, really it is." She choked on a sob.

"Janice, I'm so sorry. I never meant to hurt you."

"Bolton . . . excuse me, just give me a minute." Janice struggled for control and won. "You're neither manipulative nor unkind. You don't have a mean bone in your body. I know you didn't deliberately set out to find someone else."

"Not just someone. My fate. My destiny."

There was a long silence broken only by muffled sniffs and sighs.

"Janice . . . are you all right?"

"I'm all right, really I am." She drew a deep resigned

Indiscreet

breath. "Bolton, if I thought I had a ghost of a chance to change your mind, I would. I would beg and plead and maybe even threaten, but I'm not willing to embarrass myself or you. Lord knows I've embarrassed myself enough already." Her laugh was shaky, but at least she was laughing. "Your heritage may be half in one world and half in another, but in some things you're all Apache. When you speak of fate, I know there is no use trying to change your mind."

"How did I ever get so lucky as to have a friend like you, Janice?"

"Can we still be friends, Bolton?"

"I'd like that, Janice. I'd like it very much."

"So would I." There was a long pause, and he could almost see the deep breaths she took as she pulled herself together. "Bolton . . . who is she? Or is that a fair question?"

"It's fair. In fact, I think you have a right to know. It's Virginia Haven."

"*Virginia Haven?*"

"Yes."

"Isn't she . . ."

"What?" There was a long silence before Janice spoke.

"You've always wanted children, Bolton, and I know I've read somewhere . . . Isn't she too . . ." Janice was stumbling now over her words, too polite to come right out and say what she meant. "I think she has a grown daughter."

"This is not a problem for me, Janice."

"I see . . . Bolton . . . if things don't work out, I'm here for you."

"I don't want you to have false hopes."

"I'm not . . . I just want you to know . . ." There was a long pause, and then a small sniffle. Then Janice was back on the line, attempting to laugh. "You're right, as usual. I'm being a silly goose."

"Will you be all right, Janice?"

"I'm going to be fine. Just fine. You go back to your Virginia, and I'm going to get on with my life."

"Good girl. Take care, Janice."

"You too. And Bolton . . . I hope she knows how lucky she is."

"I'm the lucky one."

Bolton packed the rest of his gear, then turned his face west toward Pontotoc, west toward the woman he loved.

SIX

Virginia woke up filled with a sense of urgency, as if she were being pursued. Her body was tensed for flight, but deep down she knew that no matter how fast she ran, she could never outdistance the thing that was closing in on her.

Automatically she turned toward the pillow where Bolton lay sleeping. He would protect her, he would make everything all right. She started to call his name, and then changed her mind. He was gorgeous, spread across her bed like a resplendent god. She wanted to feast her eyes on him, to drink him in as if she were some parched desert traveler who had discovered a fountain of life-giving water.

She had so little time with him. So little time.

She watched the even rise and fall of his chest, the soft flutter of his lashes, the half smile that twitched across his mouth. One hand was flung palm up over his head, the other lying across his chest.

Bolton had been with her for almost a week and it felt as if he'd been a part of her life forever. She couldn't imagine how she'd ever gone to sleep without him by her side or how she'd ever been able to face a day without first being kissed awake by her magnificent Apache warrior.

She rested her head on his chest, not moving, not trying to incite passion, merely listening to the steady rhythm of his heart. How was she going to live without him?

She lifted herself on elbows and studied him. Suddenly she was staring into eyes so bright, they put the sun to shame.

"What?" he asked, smiling.

"Just looking." She traced his face with her fingertips. "Memorizing."

"You don't have to memorize. I'll be here for you. Always."

"Shhh." She covered his mouth with her hands. "Don't say anything to mar this day."

He pulled her into a fierce embrace, and then kissed all her troubled thoughts away. With the sun dappling the covers, they made slow, exquisite love. And after it was over, she propped herself on pillows against the headboard, deliberately not touching him.

"You have to leave today," she said.

"What do you mean?"

"Candace is coming home for the weekend. She's bringing a friend."

"I want to get to know Candace better. I think meeting her friends is a good start."

"Bolton . . . don't."

"Are you ashamed of me, Virginia?"

"Ashamed of you? Don't be absurd."

"Then why do you want me to leave?"

"I think that's obvious."

"The only thing that's obvious to me is that you've made a decision about something that affects me without my knowledge and without my consent."

She had never seen Bolton this way. He burned white-hot, not with rage but with determination. Everything about him was steely, his eyes, the set of his face, the way he held his body.

She shivered with excitement.

Suddenly her pillow was jerked away and she was underneath him, her hands pinned over her head.

"At least tell me the rules," he said.

"What rules?"

"The ones you're playing by."

"There are no rules."

"The code then. What's the code of behavior?"

"Let me up, Bolton."

"Not until we talk."

"Can't we talk like civilized human beings?"

"Apparently not. You don't discuss things with me, you merely make decisions and then tell me what you've decided." He applied gentle pressure with his hips and hands. "Talk to me, Virginia."

She'd known Bolton was not a man who could be manipulated, but she'd never counted on him being the kind of man who wouldn't give in to reason. *Her* reason.

"Don't make this harder than it already is, Bolton."

"These are not hard questions, Virginia. They're honest ones. And they deserve honest answers."

She'd never met a man so implacable. Today she didn't feel like handling *implacable*. Next week, maybe. Or even next month. But not today.

"All right. You want an honest answer. I'm forty-eight years old, and I live by codes that you're too young to understand."

His entire body tensed, and his eyes turned the color of thunderclouds.

"Do you think love knows or cares about age?" This time the pressure he applied with his hips was not subtle. "I don't care if you're fifty-eight. That doesn't change a thing. I love you, and I have no intention of walking away quietly. If you want to get rid of me, Virginia, you're going to have to give me a better reason than that."

"Oh, God, Bolton. I don't want to get rid of you." She wrapped her arms around him and hugged him hard. "I don't . . . I don't."

He parted her thighs with his knees and slid home. There was no gentleness in him now, only the power of a man determined to make a woman his own. The mattress moved out of line with the box spring and the bed moved two inches away from the wall.

Everything about Virginia set him on fire, the way she raked her fingernails across his back, the way she flung back her head when she moaned, the soft expanse of neck that invited his kisses, the sweet, hot invitation of her thrusting hips. His passion escalated.

Indiscreet

She was *his*, only his, and he would never let her go. Never.

"Bolton . . . Bolton . . ." Over and over she cried his name, each sound a soft plea.

He understood her needs, knew exactly how to please her, how to please himself.

"Is this what you want, Virginia?" She was featherlight in his arms as he repositioned her and entered from behind. "This?"

"Yes, yes, yes. That, Bolton. That."

The door to her bath was open, and the floor-length mirrors reflected their joining, the way they fit together, the way they moved, the way they loved. Perfect. So perfect.

He couldn't get enough of her, nor she of him. In their lovemaking there was no thought of past or future. Only here. Only now. Only the certainty that the kind of magic they had came once in a lifetime, and the desperate need to hang on and never let go.

Sweat slicked their backs, their chests, their thighs. It dampened her hair and dripped off his face onto hers. And still they loved.

"Oh, God, Bolton . . . I've never had anyone like you. Never."

And she knew she never would again. Silent tears rained down her face and mixed with the sweat. When he gave his cry of completion, she crushed him to her and hid her face against his chest.

"I don't want you to go, Bolton," she whispered.

"I'm not going anywhere." He raised himself on

elbows, and with gentle fingers wiped her tears away. "Don't cry. I'm not going, Virginia."

"Candace is coming . . . In all the years I've been alone, I've never had a man in my bedroom while she's in the house."

"I understand. I'll pack my things and move back to the motel while she's here."

"You can stay in the guest house."

"It'll give me a chance to get my notes together for that article." His smile was like quicksilver.

She curled her fingers in his hair, and held him there, smiling up at him.

"Bolton . . . I want you to meet Candace's friends."

"As what? The photojournalist who is doing a piece about you or as your lover?"

"I'll think about that when the time comes."

The time came far sooner than Virginia imagined.

Candace and Marge Rutland arrived late in the afternoon, and Bolton stayed in the guest house, giving Virginia and the girls time alone. He and Virginia had a carefully planned strategy.

"You mean you're consulting me?" he'd said, teasing her. "That's a first."

"I'm afraid of the punishment you mete out when I don't."

"Afraid?" His hand was on the back of her neck, big and warm and solid. "Come here." He kissed her softly on the lips. "Afraid, Virginia?"

Indiscreet

"Hungry is a better word, Bolton. I'm hungry for everything you give me."

Standing on tiptoe in the kitchen, she kissed him until both of them felt the hot stirring of passion. Virginia disentangled herself and made two tall glasses of lemonade.

"To cool us off. Otherwise Candace will find us on the kitchen floor, and then I'll have a different sort of explaining to do."

Over lemonade they'd planned for Bolton to join them for dinner, then afterward they would all go dancing.

It sounded like a safe plan, one that would not invite questions. Neither of them had counted on Marge's reaction to Bolton.

The minute he walked in the door the vivacious redhead was smitten. Virginia could see it in the dazzling smile she turned on him, the body language, the not so subtle jockeying to sit beside him at the dinner table.

She wasn't surprised. Any woman in her right mind would be dazzled by Bolton Gray Wolf. What surprised Virginia were her own feelings. She was jealous, pure and simple, and of a young woman she'd always treated like a second daughter.

"I've never met a *real* photojournalist," Marge said, batting her big brown eyes at Bolton. "Candace tells me you've done layouts in all the major magazines and that you've traveled all over the *world*. That must be so exciting!"

Any residual maternal feelings she'd had for Marge

flew out the window. Virginia was in such a tumult, she didn't even hear Bolton's reply.

"My, my, that sounds so *wonderful*," Marge said, leaning toward Bolton, all but drooling.

Virginia actually wanted to slap her face. What in the world was happening to her?

"I've always wanted to travel around the world," Marge added.

Virginia had to bite her tongue to keep from saying, "Why don't you start right now?" Instead she picked up a bowl of potatoes and thrust them at Marge.

"I know how you love these, Marge. Why don't you have a second helping?"

"I'm watching my figure." Marge preened in a way that assured her Bolton was watching it too. "But thank you, anyway, Mrs. Haven."

Mrs. Haven, indeed. The way Marge said it made Virginia feel a hundred years old. Next thing she knew Marge would be offering to lead her to a rocking chair and cover her with a shawl.

"Well," she said, hoping her false smile didn't crack and fall off her face, "why don't we all get our sweaters and pile into the car? I don't know about you girls, but I'm eager to dance the light fantastic."

"Dance the light fantastic?" Marge wrinkled her forehead. "Is that an expression from the twenties or something?"

Virginia was so mad, she was beyond words. Candace came to her rescue.

"That's the way writers talk, Marge. You ought to live here. Sometimes I think I'm in the middle of a grade

Indiscreet

B movie . . . or outer space." Looking at Virginia, Candace wrinkled her nose in the way she did when she was puzzled. "Mother, could I borrow one of your sweaters? I didn't pack anything except that scruffy old red cotton thing I wear around the barn."

"Sure, baby. In the closet. Help yourself."

"Could you help me? I could spend the next two hours searching your closet and never find anything."

Virginia was almost panicky at the thought of leaving Marge and her raging hormones alone with Bolton. As if he'd read Virginia's mind, he smiled reassuringly.

"We'll be fine, Virginia. If Marge doesn't mind boring stories, I think I have enough travel tales to keep her entertained."

"You're sure you don't mind?" Virginia said.

"Not at all. But hurry back. I don't have your knack for being the most exciting person in a room."

"Mother, what in the world is going on?" Candace said as soon as they were upstairs with the bedroom door closed.

Virginia had always been open with her daughter. She debated briefly about revealing her affair, then decided that what she did in the privacy of her own bedroom was none of her daughter's business. Besides, in a few days Bolton would be gone, and that would be the end of it.

"Nothing," she said.

"Nothing? That's not how you looked at the dinner table."

"How did I look at the dinner table?"

"Like you'd received a rotten review or had one of

those 'creative differences' with your editor. Are you sure nothing is wrong?"

"I'm sure." Virginia felt as if she'd betrayed the two people she loved most—Bolton and Candace. To her mortification tears gathered in her eyes. She quickly turned her back and rummaged through her closet until she could pull herself together. "How about this blue one? I think it looks good with your eyes."

"Fine. I really don't care what kind of sweater I wear. Anything looks all right with jeans." She shrugged into her mother's sweater. "Marge is bowled over by the journalist."

"Bolton?" Virginia tried for nonchalant and failed miserably.

"Who else? He's the only journalist here." Candace laughed. "Wouldn't that be great? My very best friend falling in love with somebody we introduced her to?"

"Don't you think he's a little too . . . mature for her?"

"She likes older men. Besides, he can't be more than thirty."

"Thirty-five." Virginia smoothed the covers where she'd lain with him, then walked to her dressing table and started fiddling with her hair. She was so nervous, she dropped the brush.

"Mother, you're a basket case tonight. Do you have another book idea running around in your head or something?"

"Or something. Hey, are we going to stay up here talking all night, or are we going to the Bullpen?"

"Why don't you lie down and rest awhile. You look kind of tired to me."

"Stop treating me as if I need a cane and shawl."

"You don't have to be so snappish. Look, if you're worried about our guest, we'll show him a good time. Especially Marge."

Virginia reached into her closet and grabbed the first sweater she put her hands on. "That's what I'm afraid of," she muttered.

"What?"

"Nothing."

As she walked to the door she saw herself in the mirror, a woman who still looked good in jeans but whose flushed cheeks and too-bright eyes betrayed her anger. She was going to have to do better than that. And she would, she promised herself. As soon as they got to the dance club.

SEVEN

The Bullpen was a barn that had been converted into a dance hall specializing in western dancing. It was a favorite gathering spot for the college crowd, and a large group of Candace's friends was there. She and Marge were caught up in a line dance, while Bolton and Virginia sat at the table nursing two lukewarm soft drinks.

"You're a good dancer," Bolton said. Underneath the table, he found Virginia's leg and caressed her inner thigh through the denim.

"How could you tell? We've only had one dance together and that was practically at opposite ends of the room."

Bolton lifted one eyebrow.

"Don't look at me like that," Virginia said.

"Like what?"

"Like I'm the Wicked Witch of the West."

"Ahh, Virginia . . ." He took both her hands in his. "Don't you know I want to dance every dance with you?

Indiscreet

Don't you know I want to get out on that floor and hold you close and let the whole world know you're mine?"

Suddenly her heart swelled with emotion, and she couldn't speak. She clung tightly to his hand, begging him without words to lead her through this horrible dilemma.

"I never wanted to pretend this evening," he added. "I only agreed because I want to make things easy for you."

"This is not easy," she whispered.

"No, it's not."

The line dance ended, and as the dancers gathered around the bar to order cold drinks, the band segued into a haunting country-western ballad.

"Come, Virginia. Let's be bold and dance the way we were meant to dance."

He led her onto the floor, and underneath the spinning silver lights he pulled her close. Sighing, she put her head on his shoulder.

"This is more like it," he said.

His breath stirred her hair, and his voice fell like music on her ears. Content, Virginia forgot everything except the man who held her in his arms. They danced as if they were made for each other, their steps in perfect rhythm, their bodies in perfect harmony.

He slid one hand underneath her hair and gently massaged her neck. She closed her eyes.

"Hmmm. Nice. I needed that."

"What else do you need, Virginia?"

"What a wicked question for such a public place."

"I'm a wicked man." His hands were insistent, his

touch sensual. "Tell me, Virginia, what else do you need?"

"Something that only you can give me, Bolton."

"I like the sound of that. I'll slip away and climb in your window later tonight."

"No. Not in the house with the girls . . ." The thought of a night without him was unbearable. "I'll come to you."

He spoke to her then in the tongue of his people, and the words mesmerized her. Even after he had finished, the silence was so beautiful, she was reluctant to break it.

"That was incredibly lovely," she whispered. "Interpret, please."

"When the moon bends down and touches Mother Earth, come softly to me, and we will lie in paths of silver, our bodies gilded vessels of love," he said.

"Apache poetry. My heart hurts with the beauty of it. Who is the author?"

"Me."

"You? Is it published?"

"No. Then it would belong to the world. Now it belongs to me, and I can give it as I choose."

"I'm so glad you chose me."

"Not only chose you, but wrote it for you."

"When?"

"This evening while I was banished to the guest cottage."

She smiled. "I thought you were working on that article."

"That too."

"You're a remarkable man, Bolton Gray Wolf."

Indiscreet

"And you're a remarkable woman."

They were so entranced with each other that neither noticed when the band stopped playing.

"I'm in love with you, Virginia."

"Let's not talk about that tonight, Bolton."

"All right. But the time will come when we will speak of it."

"Bolton . . . the music has stopped."

"Not for me." He grinned.

"You're incorrigible."

"And you're blushing." He kissed her flushed cheeks. "On you it looks like roses."

Bolton led her back to the table where Candace and Marge were waiting. Virginia didn't turn away from their stares.

"That's a great band," she said, trying to look casual.

Candace glared at their joined hands and her mother's flushed face. Marge took an avid interest in her cola.

"The band took a break five minutes ago," Candace said.

"We didn't notice," Virginia said.

"Obviously." Candace grabbed for her drink and overturned it. Lukewarm cola spilled into her lap. She stared at Virginia as if it were her fault, and then dashed for the bathroom.

"Candace . . . wait." Virginia turned helplessly toward Bolton.

"Go after her," he said.

"How could you?" Candace stormed out as soon as Virginia walked into the bathroom.

"I did nothing to you, Candace."

"Nothing! You call pawing all over Bolton Gray Wolf in public nothing."

"I wasn't pawing; I was dancing."

"Spare me." Candace backed up against the sink, wadding wet paper towels in her hands.

Virginia knew from the look on her daughter's face that nothing she said was going to do any good. Rather than get into a futile argument, she headed toward the door.

"All right," she said. "I'll spare you."

"You embarrassed me in front of my friends."

"Embarrassed you?" Two spots of color on her cheeks were the only signs of Virginia's anger. "In case you haven't noticed, I'm a divorced woman who danced with an available bachelor. I fail to see how that was an embarrassment to you, Candace."

"Good grief, Mother. You were all over him."

"It's called slow dancing."

"It's called making out in public."

Was she that obvious? As always, when she was with Bolton, Virginia lost all perspective.

"I'm sorry if we embarrassed you, Candace. That was certainly not my intent, and I know it wasn't Bolton's. We were merely enjoying each other's company."

"In public . . . on the dance floor . . . for all my friends to see." Candace scrubbed vigorously at the stains on her jeans.

"Spare me the morality sermon, Candace. I happen to know that Jake's mother is dating and so is Kim's mother. I fail to see the difference."

Indiscreet

"The difference is this . . ." Candace drew back and threw the wet paper towels into the garbage can. "My friends' mothers don't go out with somebody young enough to be their son."

Virginia stiffened as if she'd been slapped. Just when she'd begun to relax about the age issue, her own daughter brought it brutally back to life.

"I'm hardly old enough to be Bolton's mother."

"Thirteen years. I can count."

"Good for you."

Virginia turned on her heel and walked out the door. It was a brave exit, but one that she couldn't sustain for long. She ducked around the corner to a small hallway, caught hold of the fountain, and lowered her face to the cool rush of water. It dripped onto her collar and the front of her denim blouse, but she didn't care. All she cared about was getting out of the place where she'd made a fool of herself in front of her own daughter.

"Virginia . . ." It was Bolton, striding down the hall toward her, concern clearly written on his face.

He was the last person in the world she wanted to see. She swiped at the water on her face with the back of her hand, but there was nothing she could do about the wet spots on the front of her blouse.

"Here. Let me." Bolton pulled a handkerchief out of his pocket and began to dry her face.

"I don't need your help. You've already done enough damage."

She swatted at his hand, but she might as well have been a gnat swatting at a buffalo. His expression didn't change as he continued his firm but gentle ministrations.

"I take it things didn't go well between you and Candace."

"Bravo, Bolton. You've just mastered understatement."

Silence screamed around them, and Virginia thrust out her chin, daring him to contradict her. Things would be simple if he'd just go away. Then she could bury herself in her work and get over her broken heart, and Candace would eventually forgive her.

"It won't work, Virginia."

"What won't work?"

"You can't scare me off. I don't scare." His smile was one of those quicksilver flashes full of steel and determination. And it was far, far more dangerous than all the threats in the world.

Virginia shivered, then wrapped her arms around herself.

"Cold?"

"No," she whispered. "I'm scared." She lifted tragic eyes to his. "I scare easily, Bolton."

"Come here." He pulled her into his arms and held her there, her head pressed against his chest. "What happened tonight was a temporary setback. Once Candace gets used to the idea of me, she'll come around."

Virginia knew she should keep her mouth shut and get through the rest of the evening. But she'd never been one to leave well enough alone.

"The idea of you as what? My lover?"

"No." This time his smile was the quick brilliance of sun breaking through clouds. "As your husband."

EIGHT

Always, when he'd referred to his role in her future, she'd thought he meant as a live-in lover. Never in Virginia's wildest dreams had she considered that Bolton wanted to marry her. She was filled with terror at the idea . . . and with a sense of wonder that wouldn't be tamped down, no matter how hard she tried.

"My husband?" she said.

"Yes, Virginia."

Before she could think of a way to skirt this new issue, she saw Candace striding down the hall toward them, her face a thundercloud. Had she heard?

"Mother." There was enough ice in Candace's voice to form glaciers. "If you are through making out in the hall, Marge and I are ready to go home."

Virginia formed a hot retort, but Bolton shot her a warning glance. Funny how their roles had reversed. Tonight he was acting the mature, responsible, levelheaded parent, and she was acting the inexperienced young girl.

"If you'd like, Virginia and I can take a cab and leave the car for you and Marge," he said.

"That's a great idea," Virginia added, whipping up some bogus enthusiasm. "Or if you want to, we can take you back to the house and you can get your car. We don't want to spoil your fun."

"It's a little too late for that," Candace snapped.

"Candace, don't push me. I won't tolerate rudeness."

"Please . . ." Candace said. "Can we just go home?"

It was the longest five miles Virginia ever traveled. She and Bolton attempted a bit of light conversation, but for the most part it fell on deaf ears. Finally they settled into uncomfortable silence.

At home, Candace bailed out of the car with Marge trailing behind.

"Look, Bolton. I don't think it's a good idea if I come to you tonight."

"I won't be selfish. Do what you need to do, Virginia." He gave her a quick, hard kiss. "If I could change things for you by coming inside and talking to Candace, I would, but I think my presence would only make matters worse."

"Thanks, Bolton."

"And Virginia, whatever happens, remember this: I love you."

He kissed her once more, not in the slow, lingering way of lovers who have all the time in the world, but in the swift, hungry way of lovers caught in the eye of a hurricane.

Indiscreet

Virginia fought the urge to hang on, fought the need to cling to him and to hell with everything else. But she had to let go. She was a parent, and good parents didn't abdicate responsibilities, they didn't turn tail and run at the first sign of trouble.

She made it as far as the front door before she turned around. He had finished parking the car and was on the path that curved around the house and led to the guest cottage. The moon was full and impossibly bright, hanging so low, it looked as if she could reach out and touch it. In the moonlight Bolton looked like something she had dreamed, someone who had suddenly appeared in her life and who would disappear just as suddenly.

Virginia put her hand over her mouth to keep from calling him back. The connection between them was so strong that he didn't need words to know her thoughts. He turned around, her magnificent Apache warrior burnished in silver.

"Virginia . . ."

"No . . ." She held up her hand. "Please, Bolton. Don't come back."

"You need me."

"If you come back now, I'll do something foolish like march into the house and tell Candace that what I do with my life is none of her business."

"Maybe that's not such a bad idea. You're both adults. She has her life, you have yours."

"No, Bolton. Candace and I have a life together here in Mississippi . . . and you have one in Arizona."

He held her with a single glance. She was mesmerized, unable to go to him and unable to turn away. In the moonlight his eyes were blue lasers, cutting straight to her heart, discerning her fears, understanding her lies. A lump the size of Texas came into her throat, and she thought she was going to sink onto the front porch and dissolve into a puddle of tears, a messy middle-aged woman, totally out of control.

If he had come to her then, she could no more have stopped him than she could have stopped the sun from rising in the east. But he didn't move, he merely held her transfixed with a look more powerful than words. There was danger in his look . . . and promises too wonderful to bear.

With a trembling hand on her throat, she held her breath. She was still holding it when he turned and vanished silently down the path, her beautiful young lover, swallowed up by the moonlight.

Inside she leaned against the door until she could stop shaking. Virginia had never been a weak woman, and she wasn't about to start now. Taking a deep breath, she went down the long hallway to Candace's room.

The door was locked.

"Candace." She knocked, but there was no answer. "Candace, let me in."

There was nothing but stubborn silence from the other side of the door. Virginia didn't knock again; she wasn't about to sink to Candace's level.

"Candace, I'm coming in whether you want me to or not. It will be easier for both of us if you open the door."

For a while she thought Candace was going to re-

Indiscreet

fuse. Virginia had just turned to get the master set of keys, when the door swung open.

There were blotches under Candace's eyes where her mascara had run. Virginia couldn't stand the thought of her daughter's tears. More than that, she couldn't endure the thought of being the cause.

She made a move to put her arms around her daughter, but Candace ducked out of reach and went to the far side of the room.

"I'm glad you let me in, Candace."

"It's your house."

"No, Candace. It's *our* house. It always has been and it always will be."

"Spare me that 'two against the world' routine, Mother. I'm not a little kid anymore; I'm an adult."

Virginia studied her daughter. With her chin thrust out and her back stiff, Candace was every bit as stubborn as Virginia. In fact, she looked so much like her mother that Virginia wondered when her child had become a woman. It had happened overnight. Just yesterday Candace had been a chubby little girl in pigtails, and suddenly she was a lovely young woman just beginning to taste the fruits of love and romance.

With an empathy given to all writers, Virginia understood the confusion Candace had felt when she'd seen her own mother ignoring convention. She had challenged everything Candace thought was true, everything she'd seen in movies and read in novels about boy meeting girl, falling in love, picking out china patterns, getting married, buying a house and a dog and raising two point five kids. More than that, Virginia had shaken Candace's ideas about what a mother should be.

Virginia felt daunted. It was a feeling so rare to her that she bought time by rearranging the fresh roses in the cut crystal vase on Candace's dressing table. Candace watched her in silence.

"Where's Marge?" Virginia finally said, still buying time.

"In the guest room, working on a paper for lit class, she said."

"I'll see her in the morning, then."

"You can apologize to her," Candace said.

"Apologize?"

"For making her feel like the other woman in a love triangle."

"Did she say that?"

"She didn't have to say anything. It was obvious."

Virginia sat in the blue silk damask chair near the window. The top of the guest cottage was visible, silvery and mystical in the moonlight. What was Bolton doing now? Was he thinking of her as she was thinking of him? Was he wanting her as she wanted him? Would he always want her as she would always want him?

Candace flounced to the bed and jerked back the covers.

"You can't even talk to me without looking out the window for him."

"Candace, I'm not going to apologize to Marge, and I'm not going to apologize to you. I've done nothing wrong."

Indiscreet

"Nothing wrong! For Pete's sake, Mother. Do you think you're exempt from the rules just because you're a famous novelist?"

"Whose rules, Candace?"

Candace's quick retort died on her lips. She was intelligent and independent. Virginia had nurtured the intelligence and encouraged the independence.

"Touché, Mother."

"This is not a game, Candace. It's a discussion of great importance to both of us."

"No. It's not a discussion; it's a lecture."

"Call it what you want. I'm going to have my say."

"You always do."

"So do you . . . thank goodness." Virginia smiled.

An answering ghost of a smile played around Candace's lips. Besides intelligence and independence, Virginia counted on Candace's humor and her love to help them over this misunderstanding.

"All right, Mother. I overreacted." Candace sat in the middle of her bed cross-legged. "One time making a fool of yourself in public doesn't mean the end of the world. I can live with that. What I couldn't live with is if you told me you'd fallen in love with him and planned to marry him." She studied Virginia. "You aren't going to tell me that, are you, Mother?"

Was she so transparent? Virginia had been so carried away by the way Bolton made her feel that she had forgotten how such an unconventional match would look to her own daughter . . . and to the rest of the world.

Virginia was not the kind of woman who did things

halfway. Once she gave herself permission to begin a relationship with a man, she'd opened the floodgates and let all her emotions come pouring out.

Falling in love was one thing, though, and marriage quite another. It had never been a part of the picture for Virginia.

"Are you?" Candace repeated.

"I'm not going to lie to you, Candace. Yes, I'm in love with Bolton Gray Wolf. . . ." Candace groaned. "But that's all there is to it. I may be a fool, but I'm not that big of a fool."

"Good. He's only after your money, Mother."

"That's not true! I won't have you talk that way about a man you hardly even know."

"Do you know him, Mother? . . . Other than the obvious, of course."

"Clearly you're mature enough to have figured things out, and part of this misunderstanding is my fault for not being up front with you about my relationship with Bolton. But, Candace, I don't owe you the details. As you pointed out you're an adult; you're old enough to know that my libido didn't die the minute I got my first gray hair. And neither will yours."

"My libido's never been tuned up, Mother, so I really wouldn't know about things like that."

"Well, thank goodness for that."

For the first time since the fiasco at the Bullpen, they smiled at each other. With their mutual affection and their sense of humor, they could get through anything.

Candace got off the bed and hugged Virginia.

Indiscreet

"I'm sorry, Mother. This took me by surprise, that's all. Over the last twenty years I got used to having you all to myself, and I guess I never thought of having to share you. Does that make me selfish?"

"No, it makes you human." Virginia held her daughter close. "You've nothing to worry about, Candace. This week has been a lovely interlude in my life, and I don't regret a minute of it."

"Not even that scene at the Bullpen."

"Not even that. It proves we're strong. We're capable of showing honest emotion without letting our feelings damage our relationship."

"I don't want to lose you, Mother. You're all I've got."

All Candace had known of her father over the years was that he sent expensive gifts at Christmas. Sometimes when Virginia thought of the way Roger had ignored his own daughter, she wanted to fly out to California and smash a six hundred-page bestseller over his head.

It was bad enough that he left her; he didn't have to leave his daughter as well.

"Don't worry, Candace. You're never going to lose me . . . no matter what."

"Two against the world, Mother?"

"Two against the world."

When Virginia had something important on her mind, she couldn't sleep. If it happened to be a chapter in a book that needed fixing, or a character who needed shaping up, she could just get out of bed, go to her office down the hall, and turn on the computer. Sometimes the screen was still glowing at two o'clock in the morning, but that didn't matter because she was the only person losing sleep.

She tossed and turned, wadding the sheets in a tangle around her legs. Disgusted, she got up and walked to the window. Was that a pinpoint of light she saw in the guest cottage? Would it be horribly rude to disturb Bolton at one o'clock in the morning?

She climbed back in bed, determined to wait until morning, but fifteen minutes later she knew that she couldn't. She'd never been a patient woman, and she despised loose ends.

She threw on her pink robe, grabbed her flashlight, and tiptoed down the stairs.

Bolton saw her coming.

He stood at the window watching, and he knew by the way she walked that she was geared for battle. One of the things he loved most about her was her stubborn independence. She challenged him in a way no woman had, in the same way his mother challenged his father.

Bolton smiled. He and his twin sister had heard the story of their parents' courtship over and over, and neither of them ever tired of it. Jo Beth McGill had led Colter Gray Wolf on a merry chase . . . and still did from time to time. The thing that was so wonderful about their love was that it allowed for disagreements. He and Callie used to climb the tree behind their house and make bets on the outcome of their parents' friendly wars.

Indiscreet

Callie always sided with Jo Beth. "Mom's sure to win this one. When she tosses her head and sticks out her chin, Dad had better watch out."

"Yes, but you know Dad," Bolton would say, sticking up for his father. "You can't tell by his face whether he's going to be a summer rain or a thunderstorm."

Though Bolton had inherited his mother's blue eyes and her love for photography, he was like his father in other ways, as unreadable and endurable as the mountains and generally as benign. But anybody who had ever tried to scale a mountain in the midst of a storm knew that mountains can be dangerous.

Bolton was still smiling when he opened the door. Virginia didn't yet know him well enough to be warned.

"You need not be so pleased to see me," she said. "The purpose of this visit is not unbridled sex."

"Is that what you call it?"

"Among other things."

"What other things?"

He guided her to the chair with a hand on the back of her neck. That small touch sent shivers all over Virginia, that and merely being in the same room with him. The cottage was small and cozy, the kind of place that invites intimacy. Bolton had lit the gas logs and pulled the two overstuffed chairs close. His notebook was open on the table beside one of the chairs, and his boots were under the table.

She glanced down at his feet. They were big and substantial, a tall man's feet, with a light sprinkling of dark hair across the toes. Until she met him, she'd never known how sexy a man's feet could be. The sight of them made her want to drop to her knees and take him in her mouth.

This wouldn't do. It wouldn't do at all. She shoved her hair back from her face and glared at him.

"Don't try to sidetrack me," she snapped.

"Would I do that?"

"Yes. You'd do anything it takes to have your way with me."

"And what way is that, Virginia?" Laughing, he sat in the chair opposite her.

"See. You're doing it again. It's a deliberate ploy on your part."

"You read me too well. I'm going to have to practice implacability."

"If you get any more implacable, you'll have to hand out maps and instruction books." Though he was still laughing, his face told her nothing. It was his eyes that gave her pause. Such mysteries were hidden in them that she felt as if she were drowning.

"I don't think I can trust you, Bolton Gray Wolf."

"You delight me, Virginia."

"Oh, hush up. This is hard enough as it is, without you looking like that."

"Like what?"

"Don't you ever look in the mirror? Your eyes alone are enough to make saints turn in their crowns. And that smile . . . don't even get me started on your smile."

"I take it you like those things?"

"Yes . . . I like them."

Indiscreet

"That's a great start. You like me and I like you. We're going to have a wonderful marriage, Virginia."

"See. There you go again." She jumped up from her chair and stalked around the room. She was in such a fizz, she didn't even notice that her belt had come loose and her robe was flapping open.

Bolton caught the edges of her robe and manuevered her to the front of his chair. Then he held her there, robe parted, devouring her with his eyes.

She didn't struggle against him. She'd never win in a contest of strength against a man the size of Bolton. Furthermore, she didn't want to win. She wanted to stand exactly where she was, with her body and every one of her secrets exposed.

His eyes held hers as he reached for her nipple. She felt the quick, hot rush of desire. Closing her eyes, she gave in to the sensations that Bolton's touch created. When his mouth closed over her breast, she arched her back and groaned.

"This is not fair," she said.

"All's fair in love and war."

"Is this love or war?"

"Both, I think . . ." He thoroughly kissed her left breast then moved on to her right. "In that order," he murmured.

She wouldn't argue with that, *couldn't* argue with that. If her easy acquiescence made her weak and selfish, she didn't care. She had come to the cottage to end the affair. There was no future for the two of them, but they had the moment, and it was too precious to be thrown away.

"Love me . . . please . . . tonight I don't want to think, I don't want to talk." She wove her fingers in his hair and pulled him closer. "Tonight, just love me."

He eased her robe off her shoulders, and it pooled at their feet. Pulling her close, he tipped up her chin.

"You're the most exciting woman I've ever known." He ravished her with a kiss, and as he lowered her to the rug, he whispered, "It will always be this way with us, Virginia, love and war."

"Shhh, don't talk, not yet." She pulled him fiercely to her breast. "Love me, Bolton. Put out this fire before it destroys me."

"I'll always put out your fires . . . always."

They loved as if they'd waited a lifetime for each other, loved until their bodies were slick with sweat and glistened in the glow from the fire. They loved until the first faint fingers of dawn turned the windows soft shades of rose and gold.

Bolton wrapped Virginia's robe around her shoulders and pulled her onto his lap.

"I will always remember tonight," she whispered.

"Memories fade, Virginia, but I will always be here for you."

Suddenly she was too full to speak. One word and the tears clogging her throat would burst forth in a flood that might never stop. He rocked her, smoothing her damp hair and murmuring love words to her in Athabascan.

She was still for a long time, soaking up the beauty of the moment, committing it to memory so that in the

Indiscreet

long lonely winter ahead she could take comfort in remembering.

"I never did learn that language."

"You will."

She didn't deny him yet. She wasn't strong enough. She would close her eyes for a moment, gathering strength in a catnap, and then she'd tell him good-bye.

Bolton watched her sleep. He knew why she had come, knew it with a certainty that required no words. The interview was finished. Now there was only one reason to stay in Mississippi—Virginia. Could he convince her of his love? Could he make her believe that the magic they shared would last forever?

He had always been supremely confident that whatever he wanted, he could have, either by hard work or patience, or sometimes merely by the sheer force of his will. But he'd never met anyone like Virginia. For the first time in his life he couldn't predict the outcome.

Her face was damp and dewy from their lovemaking and the glow of the fire. Tenderly he touched her cheek, then he licked her scent off the tips of his fingers. She stirred, smiling in her sleep and snuggling closer to him. He joined their hands, and her fingers automatically curled around his. Conscious, she might deny her feelings, but unconscious, she melted into him as naturally as the snows of spring melted into Mother Earth.

Suddenly he knew the outcome, he could predict the future. Virginia would be his no matter how long it took to win her.

She woke with a start.

"What time is it?"

"Just after dawn."

"I didn't mean to sleep so long."

"I'll escort you back if you want to go now. Candace is probably not awake yet."

"It doesn't matter. Candace knows."

Virginia went into the bathroom and splashed water on her face. She didn't dare look in the mirror. Every night took its toll for the years would not be denied. They extracted their due no matter how much she paid for products with names such as line preventer and repair complex. Why didn't the cosmetic companies just get realistic and call the night cream damage control?

Bolton was still sitting on the rug with the fire burnishing his light copper-colored skin. She leaned against the bathroom door and drank in the sight of him. Even after a marathon session of sex, she still wanted him, wanted him with such hungry desperation that she had to bite the inside of her lip to keep from crying out.

"Would you like something to eat?" he asked. "I'll make scrambled eggs and toast."

"No, thank you. I want to suffer."

Her face told the story; The battle could no longer be postponed. Bolton stood up and propped his elbow on the fireplace, towering over her, gloriously naked.

"Would you please put on some clothes?"

"Do I distract you, Virginia?"

"You know you do."

"You said you wanted to suffer." His smile was without mirth.

"Not that much."

They locked eyes, and she was the first to look away.

"You could join me," he said. "Slip your robe off, Virginia. I want to see you naked once more in the morning sun."

"You don't give up easily, do you?"

"I don't give up at all. Did you think I would?"

NINE

She really hadn't known what to expect. In spite of her vast experience with men in the fantasy world, she'd had very little in the real world. Roger had been her first man, and after he had left she'd been too busy raising Candace and carving out a career to develop another relationship, even if she had wanted to. It took years to get the bitter taste of her first disastrous marriage out of her mouth, and when she thought she had recovered, good old Harry had led her down another boulevard of broken dreams.

"Scared, Virginia?"

"How did you know what I was thinking?"

"Your face told me."

She put her hands on her cheeks. "I'm not scared of you, if that's what you're thinking."

"You have no reason to be afraid of me. Not now, not ever."

"There you go again. Assuming a future for us."

Indiscreet

"It was no assumption. It's fact. There *is* a future for us, Virginia."

"How can you be so sure?"

"Fate never makes mistakes."

"I've met at least a dozen men who would have made my life a living hell. And I probably would have given my share of it to them. How do you know fate didn't send them my way?"

"What did your heart tell you?"

She batted at the air as if she were swatting flies.

"I'd be in a pretty pickle if I'd listened to my heart. It was so broken when Roger left that all I wanted to do was crawl into bed and stay there. But I didn't." She balled her hands into fists and thrust out her chin. "I don't listen to my heart, Bolton. I listen to my head."

Bolton wanted to pick her up and ride off on one of her white Arabians. His gut instinct told him that the only way he could ever make Virginia listen to her heart was to take her captive, to get her away from computers and cars and microwave ovens and all the other machines that cluttered up her life. He always went back to nature when he needed to understand the message of his heart.

If he had spent a few days in the mountains thinking, he'd never have bought Janice a ring. Fortunately, he'd corrected that mistake before it was too late.

Was it too late to keep Virginia from making a mistake that would cost them the future?

"Come with me, Virginia."

"Where?"

"Back to Arizona, back to the mountains and the rivers and the forests, back to a place where man can understand the messages of the heart."

Almost, his vision seduced her. Almost she could believe that what he said was true.

"You tempt me so."

"Come, Virginia."

Bolton held out his hand. She longed to reach out and take it. One of her philosophies had always been "take the risk and the angels come." Over and over she had taken giant leaps of faith. But she and Candace had been the only ones affected by her decisions. This time it was different. She couldn't take a risk that had such sweeping consequences for a man who had the best part of his life ahead of him.

"You don't know what you're asking, Bolton."

"I know exactly what I'm asking. I'm asking you to marry me."

"Is that your head talking or your heart?"

"Both."

He stared at her with a fierce and tender regard that forbade challenge.

"To deny your heart is a tragic mistake, Virginia. Don't make a second one."

She held her breath as he watched her. To speak now would be to deny Bolton the right to make his case. Her legs shook as she sat on the edge of her chair, waiting for him to speak. He stood by the mantel as magnificent and enduring as a mountain, as still and beautiful as a wild animal sensing danger.

To see him was to want him. Her interlude with him

was the most magical experience of her life. But could it last? Could she believe in miracles?

Say something, she silently screamed at him. *Say something to make me believe.*

As if he had read her thoughts, he began to speak.

"Don't make the mistake of thinking that I haven't given this matter any thought. I take love and marriage very seriously. It doesn't take forever to recognize the things that you would bring to a marriage. Love. Passion. Laughter. Warmth. Intelligent conversation. Intellectual stimulation. Companionship."

Virginia's hope began to shrivel and die. What he'd said was not enough.

"What about children?" she whispered.

For a split second his face was naked, and she saw the thing that scared her most.

"You want children, don't you, Bolton?"

"I'll have a child—Candace."

"I'm talking about a child with your genes, Bolton . . . a child you can watch grow, a child you can teach to fish and ride and speak in the beautiful language of your people. That's the kind of child you want."

More than anything she wanted a quick denial from Bolton. She wanted him to say that children didn't matter, that she was enough for him. His silence was more painful than words. Virginia squeezed her hands so hard, the nails bit into her flesh.

All the other problems she'd named could be overcome, but this one was insurmountable. This one, alone, was enough to make a man as young and virile as Bolton turn tail and run from a woman her age.

Sometimes silence is a sword, slaying without words. Virginia felt the wounds in her heart.

"I won't deny it, Virginia," Bolton finally said.

A primal scream gathered in her throat, and she knew that when Bolton was gone she'd go deep into the woods and howl like a wolf.

"Let's end this as gracefully as possible . . . Goodbye, Bolton." Virginia stood up, uncertain that her legs would support her on the long walk to the door.

Bolton held her captive with his eyes. She could do nothing but stare into their impossibly blue depths as he stalked her.

"That was before I met you, before I knew that a woman can be everything a man needs." Softly he threaded his fingers through her hair, then pulled her close. "You're everything I need, Virginia, everything I want."

"No," she whispered. "I won't do that to you. I won't deny you the joys of fatherhood."

"Childbearing is no longer the exclusive privilege of the young."

"I had a hysterectomy six years ago."

Her barrenness settled over her like a hair shirt, and she was suddenly overtaken with sadness. There was something magical in being able to bear a child, something that made a woman feel feminine and complete.

"It doesn't matter, Virginia."

The fraction of a second she waited for his denial told her all she needed to know.

"Of course, it matters! You deserve everything, Bolton, a wife who can climb mountains with you and not

Indiscreet

be winded, one who can wear a backless dress without worrying about sagging upper arms. But most of all you deserve a woman who can give you a child."

"You're a beautiful woman. You'll always be beautiful."

He was skirting the real issue, but she was too tired to point that out. Besides, there were no arguments that could take away the basic fact: She could not have a child.

"Don't you think I can count, Bolton? When you're forty-six I'll be fifty-nine. When you're fifty I'll be sixty-three." She pushed against his chest. "Let me go. I don't even want to think about it."

"No, Virginia. I won't let you go." With subtle pressure he pulled her so close, she could feel his body heat through her robe.

"Do you think I want people asking if I'm your mother?"

"That's ridiculous."

"Oh, is it? Have you taken a good look at my thighs? And what about my belly? When you're knocking 'em dead at the beach, I'll look like somebody whose skin needs a good pressing."

"Do you think I'm that shallow? Do you think all I care about is appearances?"

"No. I don't think you're shallow." She was close to tears now, but she'd be damned if she was going to cry. She'd do her crying later, when pride was not at stake and when dignity no longer mattered. Her hands shook as she shoved her hair back from her hot face. "This is so hard."

"It doesn't have to be this way, Virginia."

"Yes, it does. Don't you see, Bolton? This is not merely about appearances. You're young and vigorous."

"So are you."

"No. I'm at the age when women start having medical problems. I'm not going to saddle you with something like that."

"Are you having problems, Virginia?"

"No."

"Good. Then don't borrow trouble . . . Most women outlive their men anyhow. Our ages even the odds."

"I'm not borrowing trouble. I'm being realistic."

"No, you're being pessimistic."

"One of us has to be."

Suddenly he laughed.

"What's so funny?"

"You. Like all artists, you can turn the mundane into drama, sometimes even melodrama." He hugged her hard. "I'm never bored with you."

"I'm glad to know I'm good for something." It took heroic effort to keep her voice from breaking. If she didn't get out of there soon, she'd be bawling like a baby.

"You're good, Virginia," Bolton whispered. His lips brushed her hair, then her eyebrows, her cheeks, her lips. "You're very, very good."

It would be so easy to let herself be seduced, so easy to forget everything except the sensations he aroused in her.

"Don't," she whispered. "Please don't."

"Don't you want it?"

"You know I do." She tried to pull out of his grasp, but he held her fast.

"Don't fight against me. Don't fight against us."

"There is no *us*. Oh, Bolton, don't you see . . . our love is impossible."

"Do you love me, Virginia?"

"I didn't say that." His quick smile broke her heart. "All right. I love you. But that doesn't change anything."

"It does, Virginia. Love makes the impossible possible."

She shook her head, but he put a finger over her lips to stop her hot denial.

"Don't you know that when two people love each other there is no problem that they can't solve." He smiled at her. "You write about it all the time."

"That's fiction."

"Life imitates art."

"But life is *not* art. It's real, and I won't be the cause of your misery."

"If you walk out that door, you will be."

"No, Bolton, if I *don't* walk out that door, I will be." When he started to protest, she put her hand over his mouth. "Please don't say another word. Nothing you can say will change my mind."

They were still so close that she was beginning to sweat. She didn't know if her condition was caused by the fire or the unseasonably warm temperature or from her age. He shifted subtly so that their hips were pressed close. She could feel his body heat, feel his arousal. If she didn't leave soon, all was lost.

She cupped his face so that he could see the truth in her eyes.

"Nothing you can do will change my mind, Bolton, so please . . . let me leave with some dignity."

If she lived to a hundred, she would never forget the way he looked standing in her guest cottage backlit by the fire. His face told her nothing. With his high cheekbones and bronze skin he might have been a beautiful carving. But, his eyes. . . . She sucked in her breath. His torment blazed so bright, she was almost blinded.

The air was charged with passion and denial, with love and pain. Virginia couldn't look away from him, couldn't walk away from him.

His arms felt like bands of steel. He could keep her there if he wanted to. She almost wished he would. She almost wished he would take her captive and make love to her until nothing else mattered except the two of them and the way they made each other feel.

Suddenly he released her.

She wanted to say some last word, something kind and wise that would give them both comfort. For once, words failed her. Helpless, she stood in front of him clutching the front of her robe.

He didn't move, didn't speak. Finally she decided the only thing she could say was good-bye. He must have read her mind. When he held up his hand, it was not a signal for silence, but a command.

His words were as fluid as the streams that meandered through the forest, as musical as the song of birds calling out to the dawn, as beautiful as the most exquisite poetry. She didn't have to understand the language to know what he was saying.

Bolton Gray Wolf was pouring out his love to her in the ancient language of his people. The only way she could hold herself together was to wrap her arms tightly around her waist and hang on.

The beauty and the pain of his words ripped her heart asunder. And when they ceased she was still mesmerized. The silence sang around her, echoing with Bolton's lament of love.

She squeezed her eyes shut against the tears. When she opened them, he was studying her.

"Go quickly, Virginia, before I change my mind."

Turning away from him was the hardest thing she'd ever done.

"Don't look back, don't look back," she told herself.

She had gained the door when he called out.

"Virginia . . ."

Her hand was on the doorknob, but she couldn't turn around, didn't *dare* turn around and look at him.

"It's not over between us. . . . You *will* be mine."

She plunged through the doorway and raced down the curving path. When she got to her kitchen, she leaned heavily against the cabinet and cried great racking sobs that tore her chest apart.

"Oh, God," she cried. "Oh, God."

She wished she believed in miracles.

TEN

Virginia put a cold cloth on her head and stayed in bed while Bolton left. She didn't want to see him carry his bags down the path, didn't want to see him get in his car, didn't want to watch as the Mustang shot down the driveway with the man she loved inside.

She was too numb to do anything except lie flat on her back, aching inside and out.

The knock startled her. When Candace poked her head around the door, Virginia looked at the clock. Three in the afternoon. She must have slept. Pity she didn't feel refreshed.

"Mother . . ." Candace sat on the side of the bed. "Are you all right?"

"No." She didn't think she'd ever be all right again.

"We didn't want to disturb you, but I got worried when you didn't come out for lunch."

"I didn't mean to worry you."

"It's okay. I'm young and resilient. I can take it."

Indiscreet

Candace studied her mother. "I almost made you smile, didn't I?"

"Almost. Where's Marge?"

"Loading the car. We're headed back to school."

Virginia made a halfhearted attempt to sit up, then flopped back onto the mattress.

"Tell Marge 'bye for me . . . and Candace, tell her I'm sorry I missed lunch."

"No problem. She understands . . . really, she does, Mother. We both do."

Virginia found the wet bathcloth wadded under the sheets and flung it to the floor.

"I wish I did."

Candace picked up the cloth and carried it to the bathroom. Afterward, she stood in the bathroom doorway watching Virginia.

"Candace, you look like somebody whose cat has just been run over. You might as well spit it out and get it over with."

"I saw Bolton's car leave."

"He's gone."

"Will he be back?"

"No."

To her daughter's credit, Candace didn't smile at the news.

"It's for the best," she said.

"Yes," Virginia agreed. "It's best . . . for all of us."

From somewhere deep inside, Virginia drew on a reserve of strength she hadn't had to use in many years. She threw back the covers, got out of bed, and kissed her daughter good-bye.

"Take care of yourself, baby."

"You, too, Mom."

As she held out her hand, Virginia even managed a smile. Candace pressed her palm against her mother's.

"Two against the world," Virginia said.

She was sitting in her office staring at the computer screen. Virginia had done a lot of that lately. As a matter of fact, she hadn't written a single word since Bolton left. Not one. She had tried. She had put words on the paper, but they were just words. They didn't leap off the page and grab the reader by the throat. They didn't sing. They didn't even whimper.

She'd used the delete key so much that the lettering was wearing off.

It was useless to keep sitting at her keyboard accomplishing nothing. All she was doing was adding failure to misery.

She picked up the phone and dialed.

"Jane? . . . Can you come over? I'm ready to run."

"Thank goodness. I thought you'd died and gone to that great writers' conference in the sky."

"I'm not laughing, Jane."

"Somehow I didn't think you were . . . I'll be right over."

Virginia was dressed in sweats, waiting on the front porch swing.

"Up and at 'em," Jane said. "Let's go, kid."

"I don't have the energy to move."

"I heard that Bolton left."

"You can't keep a secret in Pontotoc."

"Is it supposed to be a secret?"

"No."

"Did he leave on his own, or did you send him away?"

"I sent him off, but not the way I'd planned . . . I made a fool of myself, Jane."

"Good. Join the human race. I do it daily. Sometimes more than once." Jane grabbed Virginia's hands and tugged. "Come on. Get your bones moving. You look like death on wheels."

"That's how I feel."

"Not for long, kid. Old Jane has come to the rescue." Jane let go and twirled around on the front porch. "Do you think I have a cute butt?"

"I've never noticed."

"Well, notice. Is it cute?"

Virginia smiled for the first time in three days. It was then that she knew she was going to be all right.

"I don't know anything about cute butts," she said, ". . . but yeah, I guess yours is cute. Why in the world do you want to know?"

"Old Eldon at the post office told me it was, and I wondered if he was telling the truth or just trying a new tactic to get me to play fun and games with him."

"Eldon!" By now, Virginia was laughing. "You've got to be kidding."

"Yeah, I'm just kidding, but I made you laugh, didn't I?"

"Yes, and it feels good."

"You want to know something else that will feel good . . . besides, you-know-what, I mean."

Virginia kept the smile on her face, but she felt a small quick rush of loss and regret.

"All right. I'll bite. What?"

"Spending money. Reed's in Tupelo is having a wham bang sale. After we get our bodies gorgeous, let's go over there and spend an obscene amount of money."

"I'm too far behind with my writing."

"You say that every time you start a new book."

"Do I?"

"Yep. If you weren't behind schedule, I'd think something was wrong with you." Jane marched around her friend, exaggerating her perusal. "Yep. Just as I thought. Nothing wrong that spending a little money won't cure."

Suddenly the starch went out of Virginia. She sat heavily on the swing.

"I wish that were true." She was foolishly close to tears. Would they never stop?

Jane sat beside her, and the swing went into gentle motion.

"You did the right thing, Virginia."

"My head knows it. I just wish somebody would tell my heart."

"Go ahead and cry if you want to." A cardinal swooped onto the lowest branch of a pecan tree, his coat a flash of scarlet in the early-morning sun. "Nobody here but us old birds."

Indiscreet

"I'm not going to cry." Virginia knuckled her damp eyes. "I'm sick and tired of crying."

"Atta girl!"

Virginia watched as a sassy mockingbird tried to chase the cardinal away.

"He hasn't even called," she said. "Why doesn't he call?"

"Do you want me to answer that?" Virginia waited, knowing Jane could never resist saying exactly what she thought. "I think Mr. Bolton Gray Wolf got back out to Arizona and licked his wounded pride for a couple of days, then he took a good hard long distance look and decided he'd had a very narrow escape."

Virginia sucked in her breath.

"Well, you wanted the truth, didn't you?"

"Yes."

"Look, Virginia, you did the right thing. People are still talking about the two of you at that dance."

"What are they saying? No, wait a minute. I don't want to know."

"They're saying exactly what you'd expect them to say. But it's over and done with now, and you're going to dress up in one of your outrageously expensive outfits that makes you look twice as beautiful as you already are and stick out your chin and sashay your gorgeous self all over this town smiling like you've just been crowned the Queen of the World . . . even if I have to drag you down the streets kicking and screaming."

Strength began to pour through Virginia. With a friend like Jane, nothing was going to happen that she couldn't handle.

"Jane, that is quite possibly the worst example of syntax I've ever heard."

"Hey, I never do anything halfway."

Virginia leaned on her porch railing and took a deep breath. Her land was spread out before her—the lake sparkling in the autumn sun, the pasture with patches of brown beginning to show through the green, the woods that would soon put on a flamboyant color show to rival anything she'd see on the world's greatest stages. In the distance her Arabians cavorted in the paddock, tossing their gleaming manes. It was all hers, a land, a home, and possessions she'd acquired the hard way, with years of sacrifice and perseverance.

"Neither do I," she said.

She had a good life—a wonderful daughter, a dear and loyal friend, a comfortable home, a great career.

Nothing was going to steal her joy. Not even the loss of a magnificent Apache warrior called Gray Wolf.

Bolton rode Apache style, his knees dug into the stallion's side and his hands so light on the reins that horse and rider seemed one. The horse was a paint, the kind ridden by his ancestors, a gritty breed exactly right for the kind of daredevil riding Bolton loved. They thundered down from the mountain, taking the precarious trail at a speed no other would dare . . . no other except Callie Gray Wolf.

She stood in the paddock watching her twin brother's descent. Her Jeep Wrangler was nearby, her black Lab was at her feet, and her eyes were riveted on horse and rider.

It was too dark for him to be riding that way. Even Callie wouldn't have taken such risks with the blood-red sun disappearing over the rim of the mountain and casting purple shadows on the trail. Though patience was not her style, Callie had to wait until Bolton wheeled the paint to a stop to have her say.

"What are you trying to do?" she said. "Kill yourself?"

"Hello, Callie. When did you get back from Africa?"

"Last Tuesday. I can't believe you'd risk the stallion that way."

"Lancelot was never at risk. I know exactly what I'm doing."

"Oh, do you?"

"Yes. Always."

Callie stood toe-to-toe with her brother, eyes blazing and hands balled into fists.

"I ought to horsewhip you."

Coming from Callie, that was no idle threat. Bolton had seen her in action. When they were eight years old, visiting their mother's people in Mississippi, she'd taken her grandmother's buggy whip to a boy twice her size for calling her a papoose. If Bolton hadn't stepped in, her victim probably would have ended up with more than a cut on his cheek and a bruise on his arm.

Bolton stared into a face as inscrutable as his own, with the same high cheekbones, the same dusty golden skin. They had the same blue eyes, the same tall frame. But there the resemblance ended. He was calm and creative, she was explosive and analytical. He was rugged and masculine, she was blatantly feminine. He walked a steady course, always certain of what he wanted while Callie zigged and zagged all over the country, never sure of what she wanted or what she would do next.

A doctor specializing in exotic diseases, she traveled the world doing battle against little-known deadly viruses. It was a job exactly suited for a woman with her brand of temperament and courage.

But no matter where she went, Callie always came home to the White Mountains, always came back to the land that had nurtured her and the family that loved her.

Her greeting was typical. Between journeys Callie took up exactly where she'd left off, perhaps in an attempt to act as if she'd never left home to put herself at risk time and again.

They both looked at each other and suddenly burst into laughter.

"Welcome home, Callie."

She looped an arm around his waist, and they walked together toward his house.

"I can, you know," she said, ". . . whip the daylights out of you."

"I've no doubt that you'd try."

They sat together on the front porch swing with Callie's Lab licking her ankles.

"My original question stands. What are you trying to do to yourself?"

Callie never asked an idle question. Trained in science and medicine, she had the kind of mind that sifted

Indiscreet

through extraneous details and cut right to the heart of the matter.

"You've been talking to Janice," he said.

"How did you know?"

"You're not the only one with analytical abilities, Dr. Gray Wolf."

"Yes, I've been talking to her. But not behind your back."

"I know you wouldn't do that, Callie."

"She told me you dumped her for that novelist."

"Janice said that?"

"Not exactly in those words. She's too sweet for that. She said that you'd fallen in love and Virginia Haven had broken your heart."

"I wouldn't put it that way."

"How would you put it, Bolton?"

"I'd put it this way, Callie: I love Virginia and I'm going to be with her. Period. End of discussion."

"Are you telling me this is none of my business and to keep my nosy self out of it?"

"I couldn't have said it better."

"Well . . . you know what a damned fool notion I think love is in the first place. And in the second place, you need not tell me what to do because I won't listen."

He laughed. "You never have. Why should you start now?"

"Precisely. Now that we've got that settled . . . get yourself inside and put on something that doesn't smell like horses, because you and I are going to Mom and Dad's for dinner."

"I've already declined that invitation."

"I *undeclined* for you."

Bolton hadn't wanted to do anything since he got back from Mississippi except ride through the mountains with the wind in his hair and the rain on his face. He had spent days in quiet communion with nature, days listening to the sounds he loved—the call of the eagle and the trill of the turtledove, the roar of waterfalls and the trickle of streams, the mighty rush of storm winds and the whisper of breezes. And through it all there had not been one day that he hadn't thought of Virginia, not one hour that he hadn't longed for her, not one moment that he hadn't loved her.

As much as he loved his sister and his parents, he'd needed that time alone. But now it was time for action.

He stood up and looked down at his sister.

"Wipe that smug smile off your face. I'm not doing this for you. I'm doing it because I want to."

Callie swatted his leg.

"Scat. Shoo. Go in there and get gorgeous. The world is full of women waiting to swoon over you."

"There's only one woman I want."

Callie felt a gut punch that meant trouble. Ever since they had been children, she'd always known instinctively when her twin needed her help.

She followed him into the house and didn't bat an eye about snooping while he was in the shower. Not that he was trying to hide anything. The thing about her brother that made him so vulnerable was his frank and open manner.

The pictures were spread across the coffee table,

Indiscreet

dozens of them, some black and white, some color, all beautiful, all of the same woman.

Callie picked up the first one and sucked in a sharp breath. The woman's face was soft and misty and full of wonder, as if she'd seen something that mere mortals couldn't see.

"She's beautiful, isn't she?"

Callie whirled around. Her brother was standing behind her, his hair still damp from his bath. It didn't surprise Callie at all that Virginia Haven had fallen in love with him. What surprised her was her own reaction, fear tinged with sorrow . . . and envy.

"Hey, you're crying." Bolton took a handkerchief from his pocket and tenderly wiped his sister's face. "There's no need to cry, Callie. Everything is going to be all right."

"I thought so too . . . until I saw this."

Bolton took the photograph. It was the one he'd taken underneath the trees on Virginia's farm right after they had first made love.

"It's Virginia."

"I guessed as much." Tears rolled down her cheeks, and Callie sniffled. "I didn't think it was real, Bolton. I mean . . . love. It just doesn't happen."

"It happened to Mom and Dad."

"I know, but that's different. They're our parents."

"Callie . . . Callie . . ." Bolton hugged his sister. "When are you going to learn? Love happens."

She took a big sniffle, then threw back her head and glared at him.

"Not to me, it won't. I'm not fixing to mess up my life with that kind of sentimental poppycock."

"You don't have to look so fierce. I'm not arguing with you."

Callie took the handkerchief and finished wiping her face, then she sat on the sofa and picked up the other photographs, one by one. With his camera Bolton had uncovered all of Virginia's secrets, had laid her emotions bare.

A close-up of Virginia in her pink bathrobe slid to the floor. As Bolton picked it up he remembered the morning he had snapped it, the morning he had walked up the stairs with her and made love in her bedroom that smelled like roses.

His heart hurt so much that he could hardly breathe. He studied the picture, not critically in the way of a professional photographer, but tenderly in the way of a lover.

Had time and distance made a difference? Would she listen to her heart now? Or was he being a fool? Maybe she'd been listening to her heart all along, and its answers were not the ones Bolton wanted to hear.

"She loves you, Bolton," Callie said.

"You must have read my mind."

"I always have."

He traced the path of sunlight on Virginia's face.

"How do you know?"

"I've seen that look on the face of our mother."

Bolton had too. In old photographs taken when Jo Beth McGill married Colter Gray Wolf, in snapshots

Indiscreet

taken over the years and pasted in the family album, and on his mother's face every time she looked at his father.

"Thank you, Callie."

She didn't have to ask to understand why he was thanking her. Callie slid off the sofa and put her hand on his arm.

"You know I don't understand any of this, Bolton. I'm not even sure I approve of it—and not because of her age. Janice told me, and I don't give a flip about that. But I want you to know one thing: I'll do anything to help you."

"I know you mean well, Callie, but . . ."

Callie was on a roll and wouldn't be stopped.

"I'll pick out a ring, I'll shine your shoes and clean your stables. Heck, I'll even fly down there and tell her how wonderful you are—when you're not being a pain in the gluteus maximus."

"You would too."

"You're darned tootin'."

They didn't have Mississippi grandparents for nothing. When they were youngsters they used to follow Silas McGill around the house imitating him. *Darned tootin'* hadn't caused much of a stir when they tried out their new vocabulary back home, but some of the things they'd learned from Silas had gotten them into more hot water than they cared to remember.

"I still miss him," Bolton said. "Don't you?"

"Yes. But I'm glad he went when he did and the way he did. Dying in his own backyard of a quick heart attack is a far better alternative than wasting slowly in a nursing home. Advanced Alzheimer's is devastating for the family."

Callie started straightening the stack of photographs.

"Hey, we'd better leave before Dad sends out a search party."

"You go ahead," Bolton said. "There's something I have to do."

Callie narrowed her eyes at him. "You're not just making up excuses, are you?"

"No. I'll be there in time for dinner. I promise."

"Would this mystery chore have anything to do with Virginia Haven?"

Bolton took her arm and escorted her toward the door.

"'Bye, Callie."

"That's not a very polite way to treat a lady."

"Since when did you become a lady?"

"Bolton Gray Wolf, I take back every nice thing I said about you. Furthermore, I might just call a certain woman in Mississippi and tell her how you hog all the popcorn at movies."

"You're all heart, Callie. I knew I could count on you."

"Anytime, Gray Wolf."

She winked, then loaded her Lab into the Jeep and waved good-bye. After she had disappeared down the driveway, Bolton picked up the telephone. There was no need for him to look in his notes. He knew the number by heart.

ELEVEN

Virginia didn't answer the phone. Her characters were finally talking to her, and she was right in the middle of a crucial scene. She tapped away at her keyboard while the phone on her credenza rang and rang.

Suddenly something caught her high in the breastbone, some sixth sense that told her she was missing an important call. She left Wayne and Gloria Denny in midsentence as well as midembrace, and picked up her receiver.

"Virginia Haven speaking."

"Hello, Virginia."

She had to sit down. But there was nowhere to sit because she'd dragged the chair over to her bookshelves in order to reach a reference book on her top shelf, and so she sat down on the floor.

"Bolton . . . it's been a long time."

"Too long."

She knew she was breathing because she hadn't

passed out yet. But she wasn't sure her brain was functioning right, and she knew her heart wasn't. It was pounding so hard, she could almost hear it.

"A week isn't that long," she said, lying.

It had been the longest few days of her life. In a week she'd created a thousand scenes between them, all with a different ending. In a week she'd died a thousand small deaths. In a week she'd torn her life apart and put it back together. Sort of. She still felt as if she were clinging to sanity by a thread.

Suddenly she ran out of things to say. How could she tell him that his was the voice she wanted to hear above all others . . . and that she never wanted to talk to him again? How could she explain to him the torture of not waking up with him in her bed? How could she explain the brutal loneliness? The sense of loss? The dreadful mood swings between hope and despair?

The silence that overtook them was fraught with meaning. Virginia gripped the phone so hard, her knuckles turned white. She couldn't even hear him breathing. Was he still there? What was he thinking? Why didn't he say something?

"I've wanted to make this call a thousand times," he finally said.

I wanted you to, she started to say. But that was wrong. *They* were wrong. She put a palm to her hot face and kept silent.

"I wanted to give you some time, Virginia, some time to listen to your heart."

At the moment her heart was clamoring so that she

couldn't have understood its message even if she had tried.

"Virginia . . . are you there?"

"I'm here, Bolton."

"I've developed most of the photographs."

"Then that's why you called, to talk to me about the magazine layout."

"No, that's not why I called."

She didn't want to know why he had called anymore. She didn't want to hear him speak words of love. She didn't want to remember the wonder of being in his arms . . . and the emptiness of being alone.

"Look, Bolton, I'm very busy right now."

"Are you saying that you don't want to talk to me, Virginia?"

"I'm saying I *can't* talk to you. Deadlines don't wait."

"I see . . ."

Bolton had always been impossible to decipher. His voice told her even less than his face had when he decided to be perfectly inscrutable.

Loss almost overwhelmed Virginia. What if he never called back? What if she never saw him again? She couldn't keep him, and yet she still couldn't bear to let him go.

"Bolton . . ."

What could she say that would make him call back without giving him false hope? Sweat broke out on her face, and she wondered if she were having hot flashes on top of everything else.

"I'm here, Virginia."

She remembered how he looked when he used to say

that to her—his eyes so blue, they looked as if they were bits of the sky, his mouth curved in one of those mysterious smiles that drove her mad, his hands resting lightly on her bare stomach.

She held her breath waiting for the rest of it.

"I'll always be here for you."

She exhaled slowly. Then she leaned against the credenza and closed her eyes.

"Virginia . . . are you there?"

"Yes . . . and no."

His voice stole through her like a thief in the night, robbing her of all ability to think, let alone speak. She shook her head to clear it. Now was not the time to go soft.

"I'm here physically," she added, "but not mentally. You know how it is when you're working on a project. Nothing else matters."

"Yes," he said, and she silently thanked him for not challenging her lie.

"I have to go now, Bolton . . ." Once again the long silence overtook them. Was he hanging on to the receiver the way she was, reluctant to break the fragile connection that bound them?

"Call me," she whispered.

"You can count on it."

Impossible hope sprang to life in her, and she knew she was setting herself up for heartbreak. More than that, she was setting him up for another fall.

"To talk about the magazine layout," she added. "That's all I meant, Bolton. I know how it is when you start to write something and discover you don't have all

Indiscreet

the information you need. So if you come to that point, please feel free to call me, and if I don't answer, you can leave a message on my machine. I'll return your call if you'll just be sure to tell me what you need."

She sounded like a babbling idiot. Virginia bit her bottom lip to keep from rattling on.

"I need *you*, Virginia. . . ."

Another hot flash almost felled her, but this time it was not something she could blame on menopause. The culprit was desire, pure and simple. She meant to protest, but all she could do was clamp her lips tight against a moan.

There was another long silence, and then a soft click as Virginia hung up. She closed her eyes and hugged the receiver to her breast.

"I need you, too, Bolton," she whispered. "Oh, God, I need you."

In honor of Callie's homecoming, Jo Beth had prepared her favorite meat loaf as well as some ancient Apache foods—pit-baked mescal, boiled locust tree blossoms, and cactus fruits. Tradition was important to Colter Gray Wolf, and he and Jo Beth had worked hard to see that neither of their children forgot their Apache heritage.

Their grandmother, Little Deer, had a place of honor at the table. Though shrunken by age and almost crippled by arthritis, she still had a mind that was razor sharp.

Callie was her first target.

"Tell me what you did in that foreign country."

"I helped find a way to stop a dreadful virus."

"Your father once went to a foreign country to do that."

"San Francisco is not a foreign country, Grandmother, and he's a general practitioner."

"It's not Apache tribal lands. It's foreign, and he's a powerful shaman."

Callie was going to argue but Colter shook his head.

"You should stay home where you're needed," Little Deer said.

Bolton came to Callie's rescue, just as he always had when their grandmother brought up the subject of her leaving tribal lands. He pressed a bowl into Little Deer's hands.

"Here, Grandmother, have some more of this pit-baked mescal. It's delicious."

Little Deer turned her scrutiny on him.

"Then why don't you eat it?" She squinted up at him, her dark eyes full of life and intelligence. "It's a woman," she decided.

Bolton shot Callie a look.

"I didn't say a thing," she said.

"She didn't have to," Little Deer announced loudly. "You look just like your father did when he fell in love with Yellow Bird."

It was Colter's pet name for Jo Beth, so called because of her hair. Bolton thought of the way Virginia's hair looked in the sunshine. Such longing overtook him that he shoved his plate aside. He didn't need food; he needed Virginia.

Indiscreet

"Is she a yellow hair?" Little Deer asked.

Bolton had nothing to hide from the people he loved.

"Yes," he said. "She's fair-skinned and golden-haired and very beautiful, inside and out."

Little Deer nodded sagely.

"She'll make pretty babies," she said.

There was a fine line between truth and betrayal. How could he explain the truth to his family without betraying Virginia? Callie kicked him on the shin, then shoved back her chair.

"Hells bells, Grammy, this is a new generation. Not everybody in this family is going to raise snot-nosed brats. *I* for one prefer a house where I know I won't be interrupted by babies squawking about wet diapers."

"Where did you learn such language?" Little Deer glared at her son. "Colter, where did she learn such language?"

"In foreign countries," Callie said, laughing. Then she pulled out Little Deer's chair and waltzed her grandmother around the room. "Smile, Grammy, and Bolton will take our picture."

Little Deer loved nothing better than having her picture taken. She fluffed at her hair with one gnarled hand.

"Does my hair look all right?"

"It looks smashing, Grammy. You're not a bad dancer, either." Callie winked at Bolton.

"Thanks," he told her later. They were in the kitchen helping Jo Beth with the dishes while Colter took Little Deer home.

"It'll cost you," she said.

"What?"

"I don't know yet, but I'll think of something."

"I'm sure it will be something wicked," Jo Beth said, wrapping an arm around Callie's waist. Side by side they looked more like sisters than mother and daughter. Jo Beth was still as trim as she had been at twenty, her face was virtually unlined, and the light streaks looked more like blond highlights than a graying process. "Darling, must you be so outrageous? Especially in front of your grandmother."

"I'm just like you," Callie said.

"Not quite." Her mother lifted a strand of Callie's raven-colored hair. "Not only do you have your father's hair, you have his stubborn streak. Both of you." She smiled at her son. "So, when will we meet your chosen woman?"

"Not for a while, I'm afraid. I've chosen her, but she hasn't chosen me. Not yet, anyhow."

"Ahhh." Jo Beth smiled, remembering. "She will. When a Gray Wolf sets out to court, no woman in the world can resist him."

TWELVE

Virginia couldn't get Bolton's phone call out of her mind. She propped herself on pillows, turned on the lamp, and reached for one of the books she kept stacked on the bedside table. *Beach Music* by Pat Conroy. If he couldn't take her mind off everything else, nobody could.

She tried to lose herself in the music of his words, but other music kept intruding, the music of Bolton Gray Wolf quoting Apache poetry. She remembered every small detail of him, the way he looked bending over her, the way his blue eyes seemed to be lit from within, the way his untamed black hair swooped across his forehead, the way the muscles corded in his neck and shoulders when he reached his peak.

The book slid out of her hands, and she sat on her bed fighting the most horrible case of the blues she'd ever had. Everything in her bedroom reminded her of Bolton. There was not a single nook or cranny that didn't have his imprint. Even when she closed her eyes she couldn't shut out the image of him. Bolton Gray Wolf had marked her house, and it would never be the same. No matter what happened in the future, no matter who came into her life, the imprint of Gray Wolf would always be there. Her house was his, her body was his, her heart was his.

The phone rang, jarring her rudely back to the present. Virginia glanced at the clock. Only two people called her this late, Candace or Jane—her daughter usually with a problem she considered an emergency and her friend generally with gossip she considered too juicy to keep.

"So . . . what is it this time?" Virginia said when she picked up the phone.

"It's the same thing this time that it will be every time, Virginia: I love you."

"Bolton . . ." Virginia slid down and rolled to her side, cuddling the receiver against her cheek. Reaching out, she touched the side of the bed where he had slept, long legs taking up most of the space, one arm flung over his head and the other resting on her stomach.

"Were you expecting someone else?"

"No. Candace and Jane are the only ones who call this time of night."

"I hope I'm not disturbing you."

"No." Not in ways she could tell him about.

"I couldn't wait till morning."

The sound of his voice flowed through her like warm honey. She bent her legs and pressed her knees together.

"You're working, then," she said.

Indiscreet

"This is not a business call, Virginia. It's personal."

"We don't have anything to discuss. We've said everything that needs saying."

"On the contrary. We've only just begun. I want you to get to know my family and my friends. I want to introduce you to the mountains and the forest and the rivers that I love. I want to show you the kind of life we can have together. Tomorrow I'm flying out to get you and bring you home with me."

"I can't possibly do that. I have too much to do, the notice is too short, I have a full calendar . . . the flights are probably all full." She ran out of breath and excuses at the same time.

"Two days, then. Cancel everything and pack a bag. Jeans, sweaters, rugged mountain gear. And you don't need a plane ticket. I'll be in my private plane."

"I haven't said yes."

"I'll be there at five, and I'm not coming back without you."

"You would kidnap me?"

"No. But I would take you captive. After all, I am Apache."

This time Bolton was the one who hung up. Virginia thought of a dozen things she should have said.

"I can't believe this." She hung up the receiver and began to pace. "Why didn't I tell him no? Why didn't I just hang up on him? Why didn't I . . ."

Suddenly she ran out of steam. Sinking onto the side of the bed, she put her head between her hands.

"Good grief. I can't believe I'm thinking what I'm thinking."

She picked up the phone and dialed.

"Jane, you're not going to believe this . . ."

"Virginia? . . . Shoot, do you know what time it is? . . . Virginia? . . . Why are you laughing?"

"You're not going to believe this, Jane."

"You've already said that. What? What am I not going to believe?"

"I'm going to Arizona with Bolton."

"I don't believe it."

"See. I knew you wouldn't. I know it's crazy, I know I'm insane. Talk me out of it, Jane."

"What the heck? You need a break. You might as well take it with some great-looking guy who will throw you over his shoulder and ride off into the sunset to his tepee or wickiup or whatever they call it."

"Good grief."

"Well, you called for my blessing, didn't you? You got it . . . As long as you don't get carried away and decide to stay. You're not going to do that, are you, Virginia?"

What was she going to do? She was foolish even to be considering seeing Bolton again. Wasn't one tragic parting enough for them?

"No. I'm not going to get carried away, Jane. My life is here."

"Good, as long as you know that. 'Bye now, I'm going back to sleep."

"Jane . . . wait. About lunch tomorrow. I'm not sure I'll have time . . . I have an annual checkup, and then all that packing . . . and I'll have to call Candace and tell her."

Indiscreet

"If you think I'm letting you off the hook, you're mistaken. I'll see you at the Lunch Bunch at twelve sharp, and I expect to hear every salacious detail of the formidable Apache warrior's phone call. What did he *say* to you, Virginia? I've never heard you like this."

Virginia laughed. "Good night, Jane."

He'd said he loved her. Did she dare believe that love was enough?

For the next two days Virginia alternated between elation and doubt. She packed and unpacked her bags three times. She called Jane so much that even she got a little edgy.

"For Pete's sake, Virginia. If he can turn you upside down long distance, what will you be like when he arrives? Maybe you ought to go trekking in the tundra or fishing in Finland instead of mating in the mountains."

"Good grief."

"Precisely."

At fifteen till five Virginia was sitting on the front porch swing dressed in black jeans and a black cotton turtleneck, straining her eyes for the sight of his car on the driveway. Her bags were waiting just inside the door.

At ten till she decided she looked like a foolish, eager older woman lying in wait for a young handsome lover, so she grabbed her bags and raced up the stairs to stow them in the closet. Then she caught sight of herself in the full-length mirror.

"I look like an old crow," she said, and began to yank

off her black garb. She grabbed a pair of blue jeans, a white blouse, and a bright red cotton pullover.

What if he came and found her upstairs in her underwear. He'd think she had planned it that way. She dressed in such a hurry, she buttoned her blouse wrong and had to start over three times. By the time she had finished, she was a nervous wreck.

The grandfather clock in the downstairs hallway chimed the hours. Five o'clock.

She raced back down the stairs and sat at the piano. "Clair de Lune" always soothed her. Bolton would probably be ringing her bell before she got through the first measure.

She played the entire piece twice, and he was nowhere in sight. It wasn't like him to be late. Virginia looked out all the windows, then went onto the front porch and shaded her eyes to see down the driveway. There was nothing in sight, no car, no Apache warrior, not even a speck of dust.

She called down to the security station at her front gates.

"I'm expecting Bolton Gray Wolf. Has he checked in yet?"

"No, ma'am. He hasn't."

"You're sure about that?"

"Miss Virginia, there hasn't been a soul come by here all afternoon."

She started to tell Jim to buzz her the minute he arrived, then she changed her mind. If Bolton Gray Wolf had stood her up, she didn't want anybody thinking she was sitting up in her fancy house waiting to be

Indiscreet

buzzed—not even Jim, who had been known to fight with people who dared to breathe a harmful word about the woman who had given him a job after he was forced to retire from the police force in disgrace. Falsely accused of taking kickbacks from drug dealers, he'd not only been in disgrace but in near poverty when Virginia gave him a job.

He must have mistaken her silence for censure.

"I'd sure tell you if there had," he said.

"I don't doubt you for a minute, Jim. It's just me. You know how anxious I get when I'm in the middle of a book."

"No problem, Miss Virginia. You want me to buzz when he comes?"

Virginia glanced at her watch. Five-thirty.

"No, that's all right, Jim."

Virginia went into the kitchen and made herself a cup of hot tea. She thought of calling Jane, but what would she say? I've been jilted?

"Do a reality check, Virginia," she scolded herself. Obviously Bolton had been doing his arithmetic. When he was a fit and trim sixty, she'd be seventy-three. Geritol and wheelchairs. Hot-water bottles and false teeth.

She tossed the tea down the drain and went to the barn to saddle her horse. She wasn't about to be caught waiting around the house like some lovesick puppy when Bolton Gray Wolf came.

If he came.

THIRTEEN

The storm came up unexpectedly. It crashed around the twin-engine Baron with such force, Bolton thought he was going to be sucked into the Grand Canyon. If the weather report had been accurate, he would never have taken his plane up, but now that he was airborne there was nothing he could do except fly through the storm.

Heavy winds shook the plane and flashes of lightning illuminated the clouds. In spite of the danger, Bolton was vividly aware of the awesome beauty of the storm. With his senses finely tuned for the slightest change in his instrument panel, he felt every breath of the wind, saw every bolt of light that split the darkening sky. He knew the earth was there below him, but it was totally obscured. He was in a dark cocoon high above the clouds with nothing to connect him to the earth except his instruments, his radio, and his own thoughts.

High in the sky with the unseen canyon waiting to claim him if he made a fatal mistake and the erratic

Indiscreet

lightning intent on catching him unaware, he understood love in a way that he never could have on earth. Virginia was a beacon of light in his soul. She was a talisman he clung to, a mantra he chanted, a prayer he whispered. She was his heartbeat, his lifeblood, his breath.

Without her he would welcome the oblivion of the yawning darkness below.

He was going to be late getting to her, so very late. As soon as he could set the Baron down he'd call her.

Suddenly he burst out of the storm into a sky so sun-drenched, the light was blinding. He made radio contact with the airport, then landed in heavy crosswinds. With his goggles pushed to the top of his head and his flight jacket flapping behind him, he raced to the nearest telephone.

No answer. He tried again and again, but Virginia never came on the line.

Bolton fought against impatience, fought against the urge to jump into his plane and take off for Mississippi. First his plane had to be serviced and gassed, then he had to check the weather report. Getting to her in one piece was more important than getting to her quickly.

"Love worth having is worth waiting for," his father had always said.

Bolton smiled. He would have Virginia, even if he had to wait a lifetime.

Virginia knew the trails on her farm, even in the dark. The sun had long ago set, and the moonlight was not yet bright enough to penetrate the thick branches of oak and hickory and black walnut trees that formed a deep red and gold canopy overhead.

She trotted along the path, blocking her mind of everything except the narrow trail that wound through the trees.

"Ride," she told herself. "Just ride."

Up ahead the trees thinned out into a wide expanse of pasture. The Arabian whinnied softly, and Virginia leaned over to rub his neck.

"There's nothing to get spooky about. It's just you and me, baby."

What if she was wrong? What if someone was lying in wait for her, someone intent on robbery or worse? She'd been foolish to ride at night without letting Jim know.

She cleared the trees, and that's when she saw it—the white Arabian standing atop the hill. There was no mistaking the gleaming white coat, the regal tilt of the neck and head. She squinted, her eyes gradually adjusting to the darkness. On the horse was a rider, a tall, proud man with dark hair blowing in the wind.

She had to be hallucinating. Only a woman as lovesick as she would conjure up the man who had left her sitting in an empty house with her bags packed.

Suddenly the horse and rider went into motion, racing down the hill in a movement so fluid, so graceful that Virginia knew she was not dreaming. Only an Apache would ride like that. Only Bolton Gray Wolf.

Her hands tightened on the reins as she poised to

Indiscreet

flee. But even if she fled, she could never outride Bolton, never outrace her magnificent warrior.

Hooves pounded the ground, their rhythm as insistent as drumbeats. Closer and closer he came. The moon that had been pale and hidden made a dazzling appearance, lighting the landscape as if it were a stage.

Virginia's heart rose to her throat, and she pressed her hand there lest it take flight and land at Bolton's feet. He wore nothing except buckskins and moccasins. His eyes glittered, his hair blew in the wind, and his chest was gloriously, deliciously naked.

In a whirlwind of scent and sight and sound, he wrapped an arm around her waist and plucked her off her horse. Then with a sharp command in Athabascan, he raced off with her Arabian galloping along behind.

She didn't ask where he was taking her or why he was late. She didn't question his recent whereabouts or his intentions. Nothing mattered, nothing at all except being in his arms and feeling his heart pounding against her back.

Her stables came into view. He guided the horses inside, then slid Virginia into his arms and spread her on the hay. Without speaking he bent over her and stripped away her clothes. She didn't move, didn't question, didn't protest.

Quickly he shed his buckskins, then he stood over her, speaking in soft and rapid Athabascan.

She didn't know the words, but she understood the meaning. Bolton was reclaiming what was his.

Virginia lifted her arms, and he came to her, sliding home in one deep, powerful thrust. Everything she'd believed went up in smoke. Love had no boundaries, love knew no age, love turned problems into paper dragons. With Bolton inside her, taking her on a swift and sure journey to the stars, Virginia abandoned herself and surrendered to him. Her body belonged exclusively to the magnificent lover who made every muscle, bone, and sinew sing. Her soul was irrevocably joined to the exquisite warrior who carried the power of nature in his very being. Her heart had found a resting place with the glorious Apache who wooed with poetry spoken in an ancient tongue.

He knew her as no man ever had, touched her as no man ever could. She climaxed quickly, digging her fingers into his back and screaming her pleasure. Her cries spurred him on. He drove into her, pressing her back against the soft, fragrant hay. As big as he was, as young and lusty and vigorous, she took him completely, matched him passion for passion, met him thrust for thrust.

Sweat gathered along his upper lip and slicked his back and chest, and still he rode her, bringing her to peak after peak of pleasure. She wrapped her legs tightly around his waist, receiving him with a frenzied hunger to match his own.

She scored him with her fingernails and he marked her with his untamed desire. He branded her inside and out, claimed her for his own, and completely ruined her for any other man.

The horses stuck their heads over the stall gates and whinnied while the moon tracked across the sky. Bolton shouted his completion, shooting his seed deep into her

Indiscreet

womb. She caught him close and pressed her forehead against his damp chest.

"You don't need to take me back to your tribal lands; you brought them with you," she whispered. "You brought the wind and the rain, the raging rivers and the untamed mountains, the moon and the sun and the stars."

The night wind had grown chilly, and Virginia reached for her clothes.

"I'm not finished with you yet."

He flipped her onto her stomach with ease and slid into her, fully rigid once more. Wonder filled her . . . and a delight too good to keep to herself.

She chuckled deep in her throat.

"Ravish me," she said.

"How do you want it? Fast, furious, slow, easy?"

"All of the above."

"My pleasure."

"And mine."

They loved until their passion had burned down to a glowing ember. Surrounded by the sweet smells of hay and the rich smells of earth, Bolton wrapped Virginia in his arms and held her close.

"That was incredible," she whispered.

"It's only the beginning, Virginia."

"I wish I could believe that."

"You will. I promise."

They flew out in the early morning, west with the sun at their backs.

"This is not a commitment, Bolton," Virginia told him as the Baron landed in Arizona.

"I understand."

He loaded their gear into his Jeep and headed into the White Mountains.

"Will your family be at your house when we arrive?"

"No."

"Good. I'm sorry, Bolton. I didn't mean that the way it sounded. I just think meeting your family is premature."

"You don't have to meet them at all, Virginia. This is not about family . . . yours or mine. It's about you and me. It's about our future."

How could she argue when she was surrounded by trees so old, they knew the secrets of the earth and mountains so timeless, they understood eternity? She leaned her head against the seat and took a deep breath.

"Everything else seems petty compared to this," she said, sweeping her hand around to emcompass the view.

Bolton smiled. It was exactly the kind of beginning he had hoped for. No one could be unaffected by the view, particularly a writer. He'd counted on Virginia's keen mind to understand man's place in nature. The next step was counting on her heart.

"My home," he said, pointing out the rustic two-story house of wood and glass and stone that seemed to blend in with the mountains. There was not another house as far as the eye could see. There was nothing except sky and sun—blood-red as it sought a hiding place in the western slopes—mountain and forest.

"Oh, Bolton . . . It's enchanting."

"I plan to make it that way for you. Always."

They slept that night cuddled together under a down comforter, hands linked. And when morning sun poured through the skylight, they made slow, exquisite love, then packed their camping gear and headed into the mountains.

"I feel like I'm playing hookey," Virginia said. "I've never just vanished. What if somebody needs to reach us?"

The spot he had chosen as a campsite was a leafy glade high in the mountains, protected by evergreens so thick, they could barely see the sky. In the lee of the rocks was a tepee, built in the way of his ancestors.

"Don't worry. Callie knows this place." He pulled Virginia into his arms. "I'm the only person who needs to reach you, Virginia."

"I'm here," she whispered. "Reach me, Bolton."

He tethered the two paints they were riding, then took a blanket in bright shades of red and blue and yellow from his pack.

"In the customs of my people, when a warrior covers a maiden with his blanket, she becomes his." He spread his blanket around Virginia's shoulders, then drew her close once more.

Virginia's knees went weak with desire. She'd never met a man who could do that to her. One look from Bolton and she melted. Would it be like that ten years from now? Fifteen? Twenty?

The wind sang through the pines, wiping out everything in her mind except its wild and tender music.

"Is that all?" she whispered.

"There's more."
"Tell me."
"I will show you."

He spread the blanket on the ground, then slowly undressed both of them. When they were naked, he knelt facing her, his right hand joined with her left.

"Touch yourself, Virginia. Show me what you want."
"And you?"
"I will do the same."

"There," she said, touching her breast, her fingers light as feathers. His eyes were riveted on her nipple, and then slowly he bent and took the diamond-hard tip deep into his mouth. Virginia arched her back, moaning.

Hands still joined, he suckled her until she felt the rushing heat of a climax.

"Where else, Virginia? Anywhere you want. Anything you want."

She slid her fingers down the smooth planes of her belly and tangled them in the soft curling hair. When he bent down, she wove her fingers in his hair and held him close. His tongue was sweet and tender, hot and probing. Another climax crashed over her . . . and another.

The wind wildly sang its approval, and the sun bathed them in a glow that looked like fire. The shackles of civilization slowly fell away, and Virginia became a creature of the earth—primitive, wild, wanton.

Her legs shook with the force of her desire, and when she thought she couldn't possibly do another thing, Bolton touched himself.

"Hold on to me," she said. "Hold on."
"I've got you, Virginia."

Indiscreet

His grip on her hand was sure and firm. Time and place were lost to Virginia. For her there was nothing except sensations . . . the texture of him, velvet over steel, the clean smell, the sharp, sweet taste. She wrapped her tongue around his swollen tip and took him deep.

The ancient words poured from him, part poetry, part passion. And when they could no longer endure the exquisite torture, he spread her on the blanket and entered her.

"I will cover you as the rains cover the earth, pouring my seed into you, drenching you with my moisture, saturating you with my water so that you can't walk, move, or breathe without knowing that I have filled you." He drew back, slowly withdrawing the long, silken length of himself until she was begging.

"Please, Bolton . . . Please."

"Here on this mountain I have covered you with my blanket, and now I will fill you with my seed, and you will be mine, Virginia, only mine, now and forever."

"Yes," she whispered. "Yes, yes, yes."

She was almost mindless with desire. At that moment she would have done or said anything merely to feel him deep inside her, to melt around him and let him take her on that heady, erotic journey to the stars.

"Mine, Virginia. Mine."

Their journey lasted far into the night. And when it was over, Bolton wrapped her in his blanket and carried her inside the tepee.

Virginia was instantly asleep. When she woke up,

Bolton was sitting cross-legged on the blanket watching her.

"Did you sleep well, Virginia?"

"I didn't move." She arched herself in a long, luxurious stretch. "It must be the mountain air. I need to bottle it and take it back home."

"Could it be more than the mountain air, Virginia?"

His voice was full of laughter, and she laughed with him.

Yes, it was more than the mountain air. The peace she felt, the contentment, the absolute rightness of the thing, was due to Bolton. Outside birds called to each other, and the wind sang a gentle morning song. Inside there was another melody playing. Virginia understood the musician and knew the name of the tune: It was her heart and the song it played was love.

"How would you like to catch your breakfast?" he said.

"Catch my breakfast?"

"Fish, Virginia."

She clapped her hands. "I haven't been fishing in . . . well, too long to remember."

The stream was crystal clear, and they spent all morning laughing and angling.

"Are you sure these fish know they're supposed to be breakfast?" she said.

"Maybe they misunderstood," he said. "Maybe they thought I said lunch."

"Or dinner."

"Where's your faith?"

Indiscreet

"Not in my fishing pole, that's for sure." Virginia held up a pole with a line so tangled that only the most determined fish could be snared.

Bolton untangled her line, then showed her how to cast, and on the first try she got a strike. With his help she reeled it in.

"It's beautiful," she said.

"It's breakfast," he said. "We'll clean it and smoke it over a fire." He pulled a lethal-looking knife from his belt.

"You're going to use that on my fish?" She looked stricken.

"You like fish, don't you?"

"Yes, but I've never killed the poor thing first." She rubbed the shiny scales. "Poor Ernestine."

"Ernestine?"

"Yes. Her name is Ernestine, and she probably has a family down there somewhere."

Bolton unsnagged the fish then held it under the water and released it.

"There you go, Ernestine," he said. "Swim back to your family."

With a swish of its tail, Ernestine was gone. If there had ever been any doubt in Virginia's mind that she loved Bolton, it was gone.

When he stood up and saw her tears, he tenderly wiped them away.

"Don't cry. She's going to be all right."

"I'm not crying for her, I'm crying because that was one of the sweetest, kindest acts I've ever seen. You really are the most wonderful man I've ever known, Bolton Gray Wolf."

If it wasn't the three words he wanted to hear, it was close enough. Joy filled Bolton, and a sense of coming down the homestretch with the finish line in sight.

"You're just saying that because I'm going to share my breakfast bar with you." He pulled one out of his pocket and broke it in half.

"You had this all along?"

"Yes. I'm always prepared." He unfolded a blanket from his pack and spread it near the stream. "The orchestra is tuning up, and we have the best seats in the house."

With the music of birds and the music of the stream playing haunting melodies, they shared breakfast and then themselves. Afterward Virginia lay with her head on his chest looking up at the branches swaying overhead.

"I could get used to this."

"It's yours, Virginia. All you have to do is say *yes.*"

She rolled to her elbows so she could see his eyes.

"Please be patient with me, Bolton. I'm out of practice at this business of listening to my heart."

"Take all the time you need, Virginia. These mountains aren't going anywhere, and neither am I."

They lolled beside the stream until hunger drove them back to their campsite, and in the light of a sunset so perfect, Virginia said it had to be a creation of Walt Disney, they ate canned beans then made slow, exquisite love on Bolton's blanket of many colors.

When she fell asleep, Virginia knew that she would

Indiscreet

be a fool to continue denying that what they had was true love. Tomorrow she would say yes.

The sound of pounding hooves woke Bolton. He eased out of the blanket, careful not to wake Virginia, and slipped into his buckskins. Through the flap of his tepee he could see his sister's horse topping the rise. Cold fear gripped him. Callie would never have interrupted his idyll with Virginia unless there was an emergency.

Bolton caught the reins as she slid from the saddle.

"What's wrong, Callie?"

"I don't know." She raked her hand through her windswept hair. "Mom, Dad, everybody's okay. It's not our family."

"Virginia's daughter?" He gripped his sister's arm. "Not Virginia's daughter."

"No, she's all right. She called early this morning." Callie reached into her pocket and pulled out a piece of paper. "But she gave me this number. She said it was very important that Virginia call."

"Did she say what it's about?"

"No. She didn't give me a clue. I'm not even sure that she knows."

"How did she sound? Upset? Scared?"

"No. That was the strange thing. She just said that it was very important for Virginia to call as soon as possible."

The tent flap opened, and Virginia stepped outside.

"Did I hear my name?"

"Virginia." Bolton wrapped his arm around her waist. "I want you to meet my sister Callie."

Virginia looked into eyes as blue as Bolton's, into a face with the same high cheekbones and generous mouth, at hair equally as untamed and black as a raven's wing. Bolton's counterpart in every way, Callie Gray Wolf simply took Virginia's breath away.

"I'm speechless," she said.

Callie laughed. "Most people are. They don't expect two peas in a pod." She laughed again. "That's my Mississippi heritage coming through."

"I'm delighted to meet you." Virginia held out her hand.

Callie took it in a warm and firm grip. "Same here. You're everything Bolton said you were."

"I'm afraid Callie came bearing news," Bolton said, handing Virginia the piece of paper. "Candace says it's important for you to call that number as soon as possible."

Virginia looked at the paper, and her brow knit in a small frown.

"I don't have any earthly idea whose number this is."

"I'll ride with you back to the house," Bolton said.

"No." Virginia said. "I don't want to take you away from this beautiful place. Why don't I ride back down with Callie?"

"You need me to show you the way back," he said.

"I'm no hothouse flower, Bolton. Once I ride a trail, I can follow it again in the dark. Besides, it might be nice if Callie comes back for lunch." She smiled at Bolton's sister. "You like beans in a can, don't you?"

"Is that all he's giving you?" Callie blurted out, then blushed at her own question.

Virginia and Bolton smiled at each other. Then he pulled her close and kissed her.

"Come back to me, Virginia."

"I will," she whispered. "Wait for me."

FOURTEEN

Callie and Virginia should have been back hours ago. Bolton tried not to think the worst.

"Girl talk," he said. "That's what they're doing."

He knew his sister. Her natural curiosity bordered on nosiness. She'd be bound to extract every bit of information out of Virginia that she possibly could. Combine that with her spontaneity and knack for adventure, and he never knew what to expect. They could be off exploring one of the canyons, or Callie could have decided to take Virginia up in Bolton's plane for an aerial tour of the million plus acres of tribal land.

He made himself listen to the murmur of the wind through the trees and the far-off call of a hawk. He made himself sit quietly beside the campfire and reach within himself for peace and assurance.

The sound of hooves brought him to his feet. A paint topped the rise, bearing a dark-haired rider. He strained his eyes for Virginia, but in his heart he knew she was

Indiscreet

not there. He'd heard the sound of only one horse. Besides, Callie would never have left Virginia so far behind, especially not in the dark.

"Bolton." Callie was out of the saddle before the horse came to a complete stop. "I tried to stop her, but she wouldn't listen."

"Where's Virginia?"

Callie pressed a piece of paper into his hand.

"Read it, and then I'll try to explain." He opened his mouth to protest, but she cut him off. "Just read it, Bolton!"

He sat beside the fire, using the flames to illuminate Virginia's note.

"Dearest Bolton," she'd written. "How can I say this without breaking your heart and mine? How can I tell you good-bye?"

He closed his eyes. Reading the note was anticlimactic. One hour after Virginia rode off, he knew she was not coming back. A sense of loss had swept over him, leaving him cold and bereft.

With hearts and bodies so atuned, it was not unusual for the minds to be intertwined. Especially writers. Sensitive to a degree that most people never understand, they can read the mind with a single glance. They can probe the mind from a distance in ways that remain mysterious even to them.

Bolton knew these things. And yet he'd denied his instincts. Instead of leaping on his horse and racing down the mountain after her as his intuition told him to do, he'd stayed on the mountain telling himself he was being overly protective and foolish.

A cloud came over the moon, extinguishing all light. Bolton held the note closer to the fire.

"Please understand that I have no choice, that I only do what I think is best, what I *know* is best. Someday you will understand. Someday you will thank me for the decision I've made. Bolton, my dearest love . . . please forgive me."

He folded the note and stuffed it into his pocket.

"What happened?" he said.

"I don't really know. I waited at the paddock while she went inside to make the phone call. She was pale when she came out. I asked was anything wrong, and she said she couldn't talk about it."

Callie plopped beside the fire and hooked her arm through Bolton's.

"She asked me to take her to the airport."

"You took her to the airport!"

"Believe me, Bolton, I didn't want to. I argued that she should talk to you first, that you'd be happy to take her, but she was adamant." Callie blinked back tears. "What else could I do?"

"It's okay, Callie." Bolton stood up. "It's not your fault."

"What are you going to do?"

"I'm going to find out why she left . . . and then I'm going after her."

"But Bolton . . . what if she doesn't want to see you? She doesn't have to love you just because you love her. Women have that right, you know."

"She loves me."

"How do you know?" Callie's question was

prompted by more than sisterly concern; she was genuinely curious about a process that remained totally mysterious to her.

"My heart knows."

"Balderdash." She threw her hands into the air, then put them on her hips and watched while her brother broke camp. "Hey, I don't have anyplace to go for the next few days. Can I come along and watch?" His look told her what he thought of that idea. "Maybe I can do something to help out, hold the boxing gloves or count to ten and say 'come out fighting.'"

He rewarded her with a lopsided grin.

"Thanks anyway, Callie, but this is something I have to do alone."

He called the airport to check on Virginia's flight. Her plane had not yet touched down in Tupelo. Next he left a message on her machine.

"Virginia, call me as soon as you get home. No matter what time it is, call me."

Now there was nothing he could do except wait.

"How about a game of chess?" Callie said.

"I can't concentrate on games." He sat on the sofa and picked up Virginia's picture. "It's late, Callie. Go on home."

"Are you trying to get rid of me?"

"No." A picture of Virginia in the kitchen brought back such erotic memories, he flung it away and stalked toward his darkroom. "Make yourself at home. I'm going to work."

Bolton had done a shoot in Louisiana of a crayfish festival. He meticulously developed the rolls of film, forcing himself to focus on each detail. The freedom he enjoyed of choosing the assignments he wanted was dependent on maintaining the high quality of his work. One by one the photographs emerged, spectacular shots interspersed with tightly focused, unusual, intimate shots—his hallmarks.

When he reached for another canister of the Louisiana film, he saw the last one he'd shot in Mississippi. No use to torture himself. He tried to bypass the film, but couldn't. Against his better judgment, he opened the canister and began the process of bringing the pictures of Virginia to life.

She had a face that loved the camera. In close-ups, with lips slightly parted and eyes sparkling, she was vibrant, lush, provocative.

Bolton bent close and studied the photographs with a magnifying glass. He had captured every detail, even the barely discernible mole on the left side of her lips.

The camera didn't lie. She had the look of a woman in love. Why did she leave? Why?

There was a knock, then Callie called through the door, "Are you all right in there?"

"Yes."

"You're sure?"

"I'm sure."

Silence on the other side of the door, then Callie's cheerful voice.

"I'm going to make us some hot chocolate."

"I don't want any hot chocolate."

Indiscreet

"It'll be good for you."

"Callie . . . stop trying to coddle me."

"I'm not. I don't get these domestic urges very often so you'd better take advantage while it lasts."

Virginia dominated the darkroom with her secret, seductive smile. Something inside Bolton snapped. He flung open the door.

"For Pete's sake, Callie. If you're all that hot to play nursemaid, why don't you get married and have kids."

She stepped backward as if he'd slapped her.

"That's mean, Bolton!"

He'd regretted the words the minute they were out of his mouth. But it was far too late to take them back.

"I'm sorry, Callie. I didn't mean that."

Callie wasn't so easily placated.

"You blame me for letting her leave. That's it, isn't it, Bolton? You blame me."

"I don't." He reached for her, but she sidestepped. "I don't blame you, Callie. I blame myself."

"I blame myself." Callie sat down on the sofa, her hunched shoulders evidence of her misery. "Why didn't I take her back to you instead of to the airport?" She looked stricken. "Will you ever forgive me, Bolton?"

"Hey now . . ." He sat down and put his arm around her. "There's nothing to forgive. . . ." She sniffled, and he dug into his pocket and handed her a handkerchief.

"It's going to be okay, Callie." A glance at his watch told him Virginia should be home by now. "I'm going to call her right now, and she'll explain everything."

He dialed her number and got her machine.

"Virginia . . . this is Bolton. If you're there, pick up. If not, call me the minute you get home. I don't care what time it is, call me."

"Maybe she's not there yet," Callie said.

"Maybe." Bolton dialed the airport to request information on her flight.

"That flight arrived on time, sir. Forty minutes ago."

Virginia would have been out of the small commuter airport no more than fifteen minutes after landing. Another fifteen minutes and she would have been home.

Bolton dialed her number again. Four rings, and her machine didn't click in. His jaw tightened as he gripped the receiver and listened to the hollow ringing of the telephone.

"You want me to answer it?" Jane asked.

Her hair was sticking out in bright red tufts, her face was devoid of makeup, and her clothes looked as if she'd picked them out of the clothes hamper, which is exactly what she had done.

When Virginia had called her from the Tupelo airport, she nearly went beserk. She was wearing her pajama top with orange jogging pants, pink tennis shoes, and mismatched socks.

"No. There's nothing else to say to him." Virginia jumped off the sofa and kicked her luggage. "Dammit, why, Jane? *Why?*"

"It's going to be all right, Virginia. I just know it is."

That had been Virginia's first reaction. Denial. *This can't be happening to me. Everything is all right.* But on the long flight from Arizona, virtually captive in an uncomfortable seat with no one to talk to and nothing to do but think, Virginia had become angry. Now her rage bubbled over.

"You can say that. You're not the one with a lump in your breast."

Jane was crying when she got off the couch and put her arms around Virginia.

"Hold on to me, Virginia. Just hold on."

"Oh, God, Jane. I didn't mean that. You know I didn't."

"It's all right, Virginia. You have every right to be mad. Take it out on me . . . I'm tough, I can handle it."

Virginia laid her head on Jane's shoulder, and the two of them sobbed. The phone started ringing once more, a reminder that there was a world outside the living room, a world where people didn't know that Virginia had a time bomb ticking in her chest.

"Cancer, Jane . . . I can't believe it."

"You don't know that. The doctor didn't say that."

"Ninety percent chance, that's what he said."

When she had called the number Callie gave her and heard the response, "Good afternoon, Women's Clinic," Virginia hadn't panicked; she'd only been curious. Even when the nurse said to hold for Dr. Mason, she had never dreamed she would be hearing news that would rip her entire life apart.

"I'm afraid your mammogram was not good, Virginia," Dr. Mason had said. "We found a lump growing near the rib cage."

Virginia had felt as if she were watching a movie, listening to a make-believe doctor tell the awful news to an actress playing the role of a famous writer. The actress, of course, was brave and stalwart. She didn't have shaking hands and sweaty armpits like Virginia.

"There must be some mistake," she had said.

"There's no mistake, Virginia. The radiologist spotted it right away. That's why she took so many X rays." A short pause. "The location is not good. There's a ninety percent chance it's cancer."

Women who felt wonderful didn't have cancer. Women who had just spent two days in the mountains making fabulous love to magnificent men didn't have lumps in their breasts.

It couldn't be happening to her. Not now. Not when she had finally decided to take the greatest risk of all.

"We're going to hit this thing as soon as possible, Virginia," Dr. Mason had told her. "I've already called a surgeon to arrange for a lumpectomy."

Virginia felt as if she were caught up in a hurricane that was sucking her out of her house, out of her life, out of her skin. She wanted to rant and rave, to scream at Dr. Mason and the radiologist, to make them take it all back, to insist that they call her and tell her they'd made a horrible mistake. But she was helpless. Nothing she could say or do would change the facts: Something sinister was eating her flesh away; something ugly was destroying her life.

She gripped Jane's pajama top so hard, her knuckles turned white.

"I'll be disfigured, Jane."

"A lumpectomy is not disfiguring. They don't take any more than necessary."

"You don't know that."

"Yes, I do. Myrtle had one three years ago. Don't you remember?"

Myrtle. Jane's cousin in Memphis.

"Didn't she die?" Virginia said.

"God, I'm sorry. I never should have mentioned her . . . But she was sixty-nine. You're young, Virginia. You'll lick this."

The specter of death had crept into the room. Virginia stalked to the piano and grabbed a crystal vase. "I'm not going to die, dammit! I'm *not*."

Virginia heaved the vase against the fireplace, and then sank to the carpet among the shattered glass.

Bolton had lifted her breasts so that the sun shone on them. "So beautiful," he'd whispered. And then he'd suckled them, first one and then the other, taking her nipples deep into his mouth, her nipples that were rosy and diamond-hard and perfect.

Had it been only that morning? It seemed like a thousand years ago.

Who would want a woman with chunks carved out of her breast? Worse yet, what if the lump turned out to be cancer and they had to do a radical mastectomy? Who would want a woman with only one breast? Who would want a woman who was going to die?

Tears ran down her cheeks and into the corners of her mouth, and she never even noticed their salty taste.

"What if they have to take my whole breast?" Virginia lifted a ravaged face to her friend. "Please don't let them do that to me."

"I won't, I promise I won't," Jane said, and then she crumpled.

They sat among the broken shards and clung to each other, crying, best friends who had never lied to each other before.

FIFTEEN

Callie slept on Bolton's couch, and he didn't sleep at all. He stared at pictures of Virginia until he thought he would go mad. Then he called his dog and the two of them raced along the foot trails through his property. When he was so exhausted he could barely stand, he came back inside and made a pot of strong coffee.

The sky held only a hint of pink, but it was already morning in Mississippi. Would Virginia be up? He didn't want to wake her. On the other hand, he didn't want to wait until she was already gone. She was an early riser. Sometimes she took her Arabian on a long morning ride, and sometimes she went outside to watch the sunrise over her lake. If she really wanted to get away from everybody, she packed a picnic lunch and carried her laptop to her favorite spot in the woods.

Bolton was good at his job, and that job had been to interview the famous novelist Virginia Haven. He probably knew more about her than her ex-husband.

He picked up the phone and dialed. Her machine was back on.

"Virginia . . . if you're there, please pick up. . . . Talk to me, Virginia . . . tell me what's going on . . ."

Virginia sat on the edge of her bed with her arms wrapped around her knees, listening to the sound of his voice. She'd hardly slept at all, and every nerve ending in her body was screaming. She longed to pick up the receiver; she longed to cry on his shoulder.

"Oh, Bolton," she whispered. "Don't do this to me."

"I know you love me, Virginia. Why did you run?"

She clenched her hands into fists and tightened her grip on her knees.

"Yes," she whispered. "I love you, Bolton."

"Are you there? . . . Don't do this to us."

She squeezed her eyes shut and rocked back and forth on her bed.

"Oh . . . God . . . I love you. . . ."

"I don't believe your note, Virginia . . . You always have a choice . . . I'm—"

The answering machine beeped, cutting Bolton off in midsentence. What was he saying? *I'm . . . what? Angry? Hurt? Coming?*

For one heady moment she imagined that he would come again and everything would be exactly as it had been before. They would race through the woods on the Arabians and devour each other in the kitchen and cuddle close in her double bed. Time would stand still.

Indiscreet

There would be no yesterdays and no tomorrows. Only the moment.

The phone rang again.

"I'm not going to let it end like this, Virginia. I'm coming, and I'm not going to leave until I get some answers."

There was a click as he hung up. Bolton always did what he said he was going to do. He was coming to Mississippi. But it wouldn't be the way it had been the first time. Instead of discovering a successful, vital woman he would discover a total wreck. She was on the brink of losing her breast, her mind, her very life. Even her career was in jeopardy. What publisher in his right mind would risk signing a multiple book contract with a woman who might never even make the first deadline?

Virginia went into the bathroom and vomited. Jane appeared in the doorway, bleary-eyed and frazzled.

"I heard you up," she said. She wrung out a washcloth and held it to Virginia's forehead. "Was that the phone?"

"Yes . . . Bolton."

"Do you want me to call him?"

"No . . . yes . . . God, I don't know. I feel like I've been run over by a freight train."

"It must have been the same train that hit me."

Virginia managed a pale grin. Then she saw herself in the mirror.

"Tell me that old woman is not me," she said.

"That old woman is not you. I promise."

"He said he was coming." Jane rolled her eyes. "I can't let that happen, Jane. What am I going to do?"

"Look, Virginia. I know I said some things about the age difference and all that, but who am I to make that kind of judgment? Miss Old Maid of the Century. Maybe that was envy talking, or jealousy."

"Hush, Jane."

"I think he really loves you, Virginia."

"What difference does that make now?"

"It might be a very good thing if he comes. You need all the support you can get right now."

"I have you and I have Candace. No . . . he must not come."

For a few blessed moments, Virginia forgot about the *thing* growing in her breast as she pawed in her bedside table drawer for pen and paper.

"What are you doing?" Jane plopped down beside her.

"I'm going to send him a telegram."

"Do you think that will stop him?"

"It has to."

Bolton was packing his bags when the telegram arrived.

"The answer is simple . . . I don't love you . . . Don't come . . . I don't want to see you . . . It's over . . . Virginia."

He read the words three times, his alarm mounting with each reading. Something was terribly wrong. His instincts had been screaming at him since the day Virginia left him on the mountain. He had to find out why.

Did she think a telegram would stop him?

Indiscreet

Bolton strode to the telephone and dialed. Glenda Williams answered on the first ring.

"Glenda, this is Bolton."

"Great. Are you packing your bags?"

"Yes, but not to fly to California. I can't do the interview with Clint Eastwood."

"What do you mean, you can't do the interview with Clint Eastwood? Bolton, you're the only one who can do this right. You *can't* let me down."

"Sorry, Glenda, there's something very important that I have to do."

"This had better be a matter of life or death, or I'll never forgive you."

"It's a matter of life, Glenda . . . my life."

SIXTEEN

The room was filled with flowers. If Virginia hadn't known better she might have thought she was merely stopping for the night in a small-town motel. She loved promoting her books in small towns. The people went all out, showering her with gifts and flowers and special attention. There were framed resolutions and keys to the city plastered all over her office walls back home.

Back home.

Virginia looked at the plastic band on her arm. Virginia Haven, room 335, North Mississippi Medical Center.

She wasn't promoting a book; she was in the hospital. And no matter how many bouquets Jane and Candace dragged into the room, nothing was going to change. She felt the lump of fear rising in her chest. Automatically, she reached for her cup on the bedside table, but nothing was there.

"Patients scheduled for surgery can't have water," the nurse had told her.

She was a patient. She was going to be put to sleep then carried into a room where doctors would carve her like a Thanksgiving turkey.

"Hi," Jane said. "We're back."

Jane and Candace came into the room, almost hidden behind the enormous bouquets they carried.

"That was your mysterious errand?" Virginia said. "More flowers?"

"There's a bare spot over by the closet door that needs a homey touch," Jane said.

She kept her back to the hospital bed, fussing with the flowers as if she were an expert in floral arrangement. Until the moment she had helped check Virginia into the hospital, Jane had been a brick. But the sight of her friend in the narrow white bed had been more than she could bear. She was constantly inventing errands—running to the cafeteria to get Virginia a candy bar to have when she got out of the recovery room, haunting the gift shop for crystal animals, buying every pink rose in town. The glass menagerie sat on the windowsill where it could catch the sun and make rainbows on the wall.

"What do you think, Candace?" Jane said.

"It looks fine," Candace said.

She sat in the chair farthest from the bed, her expression forlorn. Virginia knew that Candace needed comfort and reassurance, but she had nothing left to give, not to her daughter, not to anybody.

"No, I think there's still a bit of tacky white wall showing," Jane said as she barreled toward the door.

"Where are you going?" Virginia said.

"Just down to the corner to see if they have any more pink roses," she called over her shoulder. "I'll be right back."

Even her best friend couldn't stand to be around her. Something inside Virginia snapped.

"I don't want pink roses," Virginia said, her voice rising on every word. "Dammit, I'm not in my coffin yet."

Jane crumpled to the chair beside the door. Tears the size of marbles stood in her eyes.

"I never thought that flowers would remind you of a funeral."

"Well, they do."

The two friends couldn't bear to look at each other, not because of anger but because of love that overwhelmed them both. Friends since the day they shared the same table at kindergarten, they had shared everything—dating, marriage, birth, divorce, careers. But this one thing, they could not share—the specter of death. Jane had walked as far as she could with her friend, but Virginia had to make the rest of the journey alone.

"I'm sorry, Virginia. I just didn't think."

Anger boiled and tumbled through Virginia taking away everything in its path. She reveled in the blessed respite.

"It's high time for you to start thinking, Jane. I may not always be here to do it for you."

"Mother!" Candace bolted toward the door.

"Candace," Virginia called.

Candace turned around. "I can't stand this. It's bad enough without the two of you yelling at each other."

Three days ago Virginia would have handled a situation like this with ease. That was before she became a major player in the drama.

"That's all right, Candace." Jane put her arm around Virginia's daughter. "You go on down to the cafeteria and get a cup of coffee. I'll stay here."

"You're sure?"

"Yes. Go on, now. I'll let you know as soon as your mother is out of surgery."

After Candace left, Jane leaned against the wall, fatigue etched in every line of her body. Virginia wadded the sheets in her fists, pressed them smooth, and wadded them again. A cart rattled down the hall, and from the room next door came a cheerful voice describing lunch.

"We have some delicious chicken broth for you today, Mrs. Mackey . . ." More rattling as the cover was lifted from the dish. "Here, let me help you with that bed."

Jane quietly closed Virginia's door, shutting out the sounds.

"Thanks," Virginia said.

"Don't mention it."

Jane picked up a magazine and sank into her chair. Agonizing minutes crept by.

"What time is it?" Virginia asked.

Jane glanced at her watch. "Half past one."

"What's taking so long?"

"They never get to you on time. Dr. Mason said you might have to wait."

"I'm sick of waiting. I want to get it over with and get out of here." Virginia looked down at herself. The pink gown she had worn that morning was gone, and in its place was a blue cotton hospital gown, a stark reminder that she would soon be in surgery.

"I'm sick of it all," she said.

They started crying at the same time. Jane bolted out of her chair and collapsed on the bed with her arms wrapped around Virginia.

"What would I ever do without you?" Virginia whispered.

"Don't you dare try to find out. Do you hear me, Virginia Haven? Don't you dare even think about leaving me."

"I won't. I promise, I won't."

The door opened and Dr. Mason came inside. With his wild white hair and his wire-framed glasses, he looked more like a mad scientist than the genial OB-GYN who had delivered more babies than anyone else in Tupelo.

He took one look at them, got the tissue box off the dressing table, and handed it to Jane. She ripped off a piece and handed it to Virginia.

"It will just be a little while, now, Virginia."

"Good." She wiped her face and blew her nose. "I'm tired of waiting. I just want to get it over with."

"The surgeon will be in to talk with you, but I wanted to see you first. There will be a pathologist in surgery. If he thinks this thing is malignant, I want your permission to go ahead and do a radical."

Wasn't it enough that they wanted to cut chunks out of her? Now they were talking about cutting off her breast . . . and they wanted her permission.

Indiscreet

"Can he tell by looking?" she asked.

"Not with a hundred percent accuracy. It takes lab tests to do that."

"How long will the tests take?"

"Three days. Three days that could be very important to you, Virginia."

Three more days of waiting, three more days of the agony of not knowing, three more days in hell. But it was a hell preferable to the alternative, waking with her breast gone.

"No," she said. "I won't sign."

"Virginia, it would be easier for you to do everything while you're still under anesthesia. Dr. Wayne is a very good pathologist. He'll know as soon as he sees this thing . . ."

"What if he's wrong? What if he makes a mistake? Has he ever made a mistake?"

"We're all human, Virginia."

"I'm not going to sign. Three days won't make that much difference, and if they do, that's a risk I'll just have to take."

"All right, Virginia. We'll do a frozen section. I know you too well to argue with you." Dr. Mason smiled. "Nobody would be that foolhardy."

Suddenly Virginia thought of the one man who was—Bolton Gray Wolf. Call him foolhardy, call him stubborn, call him courageous. He had stood up to her, argued with her, fought for the right to love her.

Where was he now? If he knew what was happening, would he still fight for her?

Foolish question. Foolish hope. Virginia forced

thoughts of Bolton aside. She needed every ounce of her energy, both mental and physical, to deal with what lay ahead.

"No," she said. "Nobody would be that foolhardy."

Dr. Mason patted the sheet that covered her arm. "I'll see you back here in a few hours."

"Couldn't we meet somewhere else, Doc? Paris? London?"

"Atta girl, Virginia. Chin up."

No sooner had he left than they heard the gurney being wheeled toward her room. A strange calm settled over Virginia.

"This is it, kid," she said to Jane.

"I know." Jane squeezed her hand.

"I don't want you worrying."

"I won't," Jane said, her voice muffled by the tissue she held to her nose.

"You never could lie worth a flip."

"Neither could you."

The sounds were closer now, right outside the door. Any minute Virginia would begin her long journey . . . alone.

"Jane, do you believe in prayer?"

"I don't *not* believe it."

The door swung open and the bed that would bear her away came into view.

"Say a prayer for me," she whispered.

SEVENTEEN

Bolton had flown the distance from Arizona to Mississippi without incident, and now Virginia's security guard wouldn't let him through the gate.

"Sorry, sir. No visitors."

"You remember me, don't you, Jim?"

"I sure do. Hard to forget that face."

"She's not expecting me, but I'm sure if you call the house, she'll tell you to let me in."

Jim shook his head. "Sorry, sir."

Bolton had expected resistance from Virginia, but never from Jim. He knew the kind of security system she had. It was formidable but not impregnable. The wall would present no challenge to a man who had scaled mountains.

Still, breaking and entering was not the ideal way to approach Virginia Haven.

"I could lie to you, Jim. I could tell you that I had

come back to finish the interview with Virginia. But I won't do that."

"Thank you, sir."

"Instead I'm going to tell you why I want to see her and why I won't leave until I do."

He had Jim's attention, but that was all. Bolton had been reading body language for many years, and if he read Jim correctly, the old man had no intention of being persuaded. Still, it was worth a try.

"I love Virginia, and I want her to be my wife. I believe she loves me, too, but it's going to take a while to convince her that we can have a good future together." Bolton made an eloquent gesture, hands out, palms up. "I have nothing to hide, Jim. I'm just a simple man in love with the most wonderful woman in the world."

Jim fiddled with the ring of keys on his belt, then cleared his throat.

"I guess I shouldn't tell you this."

The cold fingers of premonition squeezed Bolton's chest.

"Tell me what, Jim?"

"Miss Virginia's not here."

"I don't mind waiting. When will she be back?"

"Lordy, Lordy, I wish I knew . . ." Jim coughed, then pulled out a red bandanna and blew his nose. "Miss Virginia's in the hospital."

Bolton broke all the speed limits. At the hospital he had no trouble finding out Virginia's room number, but

Indiscreet

that was all he knew. It was the things he didn't know that nearly drove him mad.

Too anxious to wait for the elevator, he raced up the stairs two at a time. The door to room 335 was slightly ajar. He paused to mentally gear himself for the sight of his beloved Virginia in a hospital bed, and then he strode through.

"Bolton!" Jane put her hand over her chest. "You nearly scared me to death."

He glanced from Jane to the bed. It was empty, the sheets tightly tucked and smooth.

"Where's Virginia?"

"Sit down, Bolton."

Everything about Jane set off alarm bells, her haggard face, her slumped shoulders, her red-rimmed eyes. He pulled the chair away from the wall and sat facing her.

"Where's Virginia?"

"In surgery."

"Why?" Jane stared at him, her face bleak. "I want to know everything, Jane. Don't leave out the smallest detail."

"Do you love her, Bolton?"

"Yes, Jane. I love her. She's my heart, my soul, my very life."

"All right, then." Jane drew a deep breath. "This is really Virginia's place to tell you, but I don't care, I'm doing what I think is best. . . . Don't you think I ought to do what I think is best for the friend I love so much that if anything happens to her I won't be worth a hill of beans, ever again?"

"Yes."

As the story unfolded, Bolton understood why Virginia had fled from the mountain, understood why she had refused his calls, why she had sent the telegram. Loving her so much that their souls were connected, he knew her fear, felt her pain.

Why, Virginia? his mind screamed. *Why wouldn't you tell me? Why wouldn't you let me be here for you?*

"That's about it, Bolton," Jane said, concluding her story. "The bottom line here is that my best friend may have cancer. If this makes a difference to you, leave now, before Virginia comes back."

Cancer. The word weighed Bolton down so that he could hardly move. How could he fight an enemy so insidious?

"No," he said, as if with one word he could deny that he might lose the woman he'd searched for all his life. Surely fate would not be that cruel.

Virginia's first awareness was of the chill.

"I'm cold," she whispered, her eyes so heavy, she couldn't hold them open.

She felt a warm blanket being spread over her legs and tucked gently under her chin.

"Is that better?"

The voice was deep and musical, a male voice. So like Bolton's, she thought. So very much like Bolton's.

"Hmmm," she said, snuggling under the covers. "Much."

"Do you need anything else?"

Indiscreet

Bolton. I need Bolton. Did she actually say those words? Or did she just think them?

A large warm hand closed around hers. So comforting. So strong. Virginia held on.

When she woke up she'd have to thank Dr. Mason for being so kind . . . if she ever woke up.

She felt the hand on her forehead smoothing back her hair.

"I'm tired," she whispered.

"Rest, my love, just rest."

Why was Dr. Mason calling her his love? Or was she dreaming? He was caressing her cheeks now, and murmuring to her in some strange and beautiful language. She felt as if she were on the mountaintop with Bolton, lying on his blanket, and listening to the sound of his voice. If she was dreaming, she didn't want to wake up.

There was a sound of running water. Was it the mountain stream where Bolton had released her fish?

No, that wasn't right. She had left the mountain. She would never see him again. The tears were hot on her face.

"Don't cry, Virginia. I'm here."

Dr. Mason gently wiped her cheeks. She'd have to reward his kindness by taking him and his wife out to dinner.

"Mother . . . Can you hear me?" Candace needed her, but she barely had enough energy for herself. "How do you feel, Mother? Does it hurt?"

Why was her daughter asking her that question? Why should she hurt? She drifted back to the mountaintop, back to the stream where the sound of water gurgling over stones mingled with the sound of wind in the trees lulled her into a sense of peace unlike any she had ever known. The murmur of voices came to her from a long way off—Jane's quiet reassuring tones and Candace's husky questions.

Virginia held on to the big, warm hand, anchoring herself to that source of comfort and strength.

"Virginia, open your eyes and look at me." A brisk masculine voice. Dr. Mason. Why was he being so curt? She preferred his gentle bedside manner to this intrusive noise that disturbed her rest.

"Come on, Virginia. Time to wake up. You can do it."

Her eyelids were heavy and uncooperative, and she had to fight off the desire to sleep. Slowly she forced her eyes open.

There was a face near hers, a dear, familiar face, and for a moment she thought she'd conjured him up. Then he smiled . . . and her heart shattered into a thousand pieces.

"Hello, Virginia."

"Bolton . . ."

Everybody started talking at once—Candace, Jane, Dr. Mason—but the only person she saw was Bolton Gray Wolf, the only person she heard was her beloved Apache warrior.

Bending down, he kissed her softly on the lips.

"Don't talk, don't even think, Virginia. Just know that I am here and that I love you."

She hadn't dreamed him. His was the hand she'd

Indiscreet

held, his the voice that had comforted her, his the lips that had soothed her.

Suddenly, she was aware of the tight bandage around her breast, of the pain, of an overwhelming sense of loss. Her lips formed a protest, but he kissed it away.

"Later, Virginia," he whispered. "We can talk later."

Then he was gone, a magnificent man glowing with strength and vitality, a man now completely out of her league and out of her reach. She had many lonely days ahead to think about that, but right now she had to concentrate all her energy on fighting a battle against the hateful enemy that had invaded her body.

"You came through the surgery just fine, Virginia," Dr. Mason said.

She felt the bandage around her chest. It was pulled tight, flattening her so that she felt as if she had no breast at all. Panic set in.

"They didn't take my breast?" She grabbed his hand. "Dr. Mason, did they take my breast?"

"Relax, Virginia. Dr. Davidson did only the lumpectomy."

"Was it . . ." *Cancer.* She couldn't make herself say the word.

"The lab results on the frozen section will be back in about three days. I'll let you know as soon as I hear. Meantime, you can go home where you'll be more comfortable."

"How soon?" Jane asked.

"If she has no problems, about four hours."

"You're sure it's safe?" Candace said.

"Absolutely. After you get home, if you have any questions or if anything unusual develops, call me." He patted Virginia's hand. "You did great, Virginia. The nurse will be in to give you instructions before you leave."

Dr. Mason left the three women staring at each other, speechless with the fear that still nagged at them all. Virginia fumbled at her bedside table for water, and Jane came over to pour it for her. Candace moved the glass menagerie from the windowsill to the shelf that held the television, then back again. Keeping busy, all of them.

"I can't stand this not knowing," Candace burst out. "I thought he said the pathologist could tell by looking. Why didn't somebody ask him what the pathologist thought?"

If looks could kill, Jane's would have felled Candace in her tracks.

"I'm just saying what's on all our minds. Why didn't we ask?"

Virginia placed her hand over the bandage. "Because I don't want to know."

She just wanted to float off in limbo and stay until all this was over.

"I just want it all to be over," she whispered.

"It will," Jane said. "Soon."

Virginia believed Jane because she had to, because believing that it was not going to be over soon would drive her mad. She lay against the pillows, exhausted.

"Did Bolton leave?" she asked.

The door opened, and he came into the room, bringing with him hope and memories too wonderful . . . and too painful to bear.

"No," he said. "I'm not leaving you, Virginia. Not now, not ever."

EIGHTEEN

Virginia knew she should send Bolton away, but she didn't have the heart, nor the energy. Besides that, his quiet strength gave her a comfort she couldn't get from Jane or from Candace. If she could hold on to him, then maybe everything would be all right.

"I'm glad you're here, Bolton," Jane said.

"Thank you, Jane."

How easy he was with people, Virginia thought. It was a natural ease born partially of his experience as a photojournalist but primarily of his innate kindness and generosity of spirit.

Candace was not as comfortable with their visitor as Jane. The flush on her cheeks and the nervous movements of her hands gave her away. She cleared her throat.

"I . . . uh . . . I'm glad too," she finally said.

"That means a lot to me, Candace."

"The last time you were here I was pretty rotten to you, and I apologize."

"Apology accepted."

"All of a sudden, I'm starving." Jane grabbed her purse. "Candace, let's go down to the cafeteria and get a bite."

"I already . . ." Jane gave her a look, and she blushed. "Okay. See you in a little while, Mother."

Virginia was too exhausted to protest about Jane's obvious scheme. After the door closed behind them, Bolton came to her bedside and smoothed back her hair.

"I don't want you to feel uncomfortable alone in my presence, Virginia. You've been through a tough ordeal, and I have no intention of making it worse by saying things that might upset you."

"Good." She closed her eyes, and he sat in the chair beside her and took her hand. "Bolton . . . thanks for leaving me alone with Jane and Candace when Dr. Mason came."

"That was a private conversation about something very personal and very painful. If there is anything you want me to know, you'll tell me."

"Don't take this as any indication that I've changed my mind . . . but you are the most wonderful man I've ever known."

He smiled. "I don't expect an easy victory with you, Virginia. But make no mistake, I do expect victory." He gently squeezed her hand. "Rest now. You need to build your strength."

"I think I will close my eyes for just a little while."

It felt so good to hold his hand, to know that he was there watching over her.

While she slept Bolton prayed. Silently he invoked the gentle Father Creator to spread his great wings of comfort and healing over the beautiful fragile woman who lay in the narrow hospital bed. In the language of the Apache he asked the Great Spirit of his people to imbue Virginia with the strength of the bear and to lift her on wings of eagles so that she might once again soar.

He asked guidance for himself, as well. The wisdom of his ancestor Cochise, Chiricahua Apache Chief, flowed through him, and he poured out his petition in Athabascan.

"Great Spirit, when I ask my beloved for her hand, grant that I may speak straight so that my words will go as sunlight into her heart."

A kind of peace settled over him, and on the bed Virginia smiled in her sleep. Bolton kept watch, and after a while Jane and Candace tiptoed into the room to take up their silent vigil.

When the nurse came Virginia was still sleeping. She quietly instructed them about the patient's care.

"I'll bring a wheelchair now," the nurse said, "and you can take her home."

"She won't need a wheelchair," Bolton said.

He lifted Virginia so tenderly that she never woke up, not even when they got into Jane's car. She didn't open her eyes until he was on the staircase that led to her bedroom. She was vividly aware of Bolton's arms around her and his fiercely possessive stare.

For a moment she thought they had just met, and he

was taking her upstairs to make wild passionate love to her. A twinge of pain and the tight bandage around her breast reminded her that she had neither the body nor the energy to arouse passion in anyone, let alone a man as virile as Bolton Gray Wolf.

If she'd had the strength, she would have kicked something. Hard.

"Put me down," she snapped. "I can walk."

"You're stronger, I see," Bolton said, smiling as he continued his march to her bedroom.

"I said put me down. Where are Jane and Candace?"

"In the kitchen, preparing food."

Just ahead her bedroom door yawned like the jaws of hell . . . or of heaven. She couldn't bear seeing Bolton in that intimate setting again, couldn't bear seeing him in the mirrors that had once reflected their erotic joining.

"This is as far as you go," she said.

His arms tightened around her and his stride never faltered. As he stepped over the threshold of her private domain, memories burned through her, and she hid her hot face against his chest.

"Here you are, Virginia," he said as he lowered her to the cool sheets. "Our playground."

"It's no longer our playground."

"It will be." He pulled the covers over her, then spent an inordinate amount of time arranging them.

She was too selfish to tell him to stop. For a little while she let herself enjoy the feel of his hands on her body. He smoothed the sheets over her legs from ankle to thigh. Memories assailed her as he caressed her inner thigh, sweet, sexy memories that brought tears to her eyes.

Would she ever again know the joy of pure carnal desire? Would she ever again feel the quick, hot clenching as Bolton slid into her?

"Leave," she whispered. "Please leave."

"Until morning, Virginia." He kissed her softly on the lips.

Tall and handsome, he walked toward her door. He took her breath away, and she didn't find her tongue until he got to the door.

"Where will you stay?"

"I'll check into a hotel."

Let him go, her mind said, but her heart told her differently.

"There's no need for that," she said. "Since you've come all this way, the least I can do is offer the guest cottage to you."

"I accept." His smile was there and gone, the same fleeting smile she had found so appealing when they had first met.

What did that smile mean? She had plenty of time to ponder it.

Bolton had barely left when Candace and Jane came into the room, bringing armloads of roses and the glass menagerie. They fussed over the arrangement of roses until Virginia told them both to sit down.

"I need to go down to my room to study, anyhow," Candace said.

"I want you to go back tomorrow," Virginia said.

Indiscreet

"There's no need for you to miss classes hanging around here."

"But, Mother, what about you?"

"I'll take care of her," Jane said. "Don't you worry."

"I don't need taking care of," Virginia snapped.

Candace shot Jane a helpless look, and Jane grinned.

"Just let her try to run me off," she said.

Virginia was too tired to argue. Jane settled onto the chaise longue with Virginia's latest novel, and she drifted into a restless sleep.

A couple of hours later, Virginia jolted awake and reached for her robe. Jane was on her feet immediately.

"Where do you think you're going?" she asked, snatching the robe from Virginia.

"To the bathroom."

"Oh . . ." Looking chagrined, Jane helped her into the robe.

"Why don't you go on home, Jane. You're exhausted."

"You need me, and I'm staying."

A wave of pain hit Virginia, and her hand shook as she took a painkiller. In a little while the physical pain would be gone, but not the emotional agony, not the harsh mental anguish that made her want to scream and kick furniture.

"I don't need you hovering over me. I'm not some sick old woman." The minute the words were out of her mouth, Virginia regretted them. She reached for Jane, and they ended up in each other's arms. "How can you put up with me?" she whispered.

"I need you, Virginia," Jane said. "I need to be here

because I love you too much to leave. If that makes me selfish, so be it."

They leaned back and looked at each other, and Virginia smiled.

"Help me to the bathroom, Jane."

"Lean on me."

When Virginia was back in bed, Jane fluffed the pillows and smoothed the covers.

"Now, how about a nice hot bowl of chicken soup. Grandma's remedy."

Virginia glanced at the clock. "It's almost ten."

"You have to keep up your strength."

"If soup will give me strength, bring a bowl. When did you have time to make Grandma's soup?"

"I cheated. This is out of a can, but I'm going to add garlic."

"To keep away vampires?"

"And insistent Apache lovers."

"Nothing will keep Bolton away."

"Do you want him to go away, Virginia?"

Through the window Virginia could see a light in the cottage. What was Bolton doing? The last time she'd seen him in that cottage he had been standing beside the fire magnificently naked.

A jolt of pure carnal desire hit Virginia. She was so astonished that she gasped.

"Virginia . . . what's wrong?"

"Nothing . . ." For a moment she reveled in the feeling she thought she might never have again, and then reality crashed down on her. What good would it do her to feel desire when she was no longer desirable?

"Nothing at all, Jane. I'm hungry for that soup."

When Jane came back she was bearing two bowls of soup, two glasses of milk, and an assortment of candy bars.

"To get us through the night," she said, plopping into a chair beside the bed. She opened a Hershey's bar with almonds, broke it in two, and gave Virginia the largest piece. "Here, food for the soul. You never did answer my question."

"I don't know the answer." Virginia bit into the candy, allowing herself the luxury of high-calorie, high-fat chocolate because she needed self-indulgence. "Logically I know he should go back to Arizona and forget about me. Right?"

Jane merely smiled, then peeled the wrapper off another candy bar and began munching.

"All that chocolate is not good for you," Virginia said. She picked up her soupspoon, but after two bites she couldn't keep up the pretense of normality.

"How much of my breast do you think they took?"

"Not much."

"You don't know that, do you? Did Dr. Mason say that?"

"No. It's just a gut feeling."

Virginia shoved her food aside and climbed out of bed.

"I can't stand this anymore. I have to know."

"What are you doing?" Jane said, following her into the bathroom.

Virginia rummaged in a drawer until she found a pair of scissors.

"I'm going to find out."

"You can't do that," Jane said.

Ignoring her, Virginia eased the scissors underneath the tape.

"Virginia . . . stop that. You're going to cut yourself."

"I've already been cut."

"Oh, hell . . . give me the scissors." Jane began the delicate procedure of cutting away Virginia's bandage. "I haven't cussed since New Year's Day of 1990. You're driving me crazy . . ." She gingerly peeled away the first layer of Virginia's bandage. "It's a damned good thing I took a serious first-aid course and know my fanny from a hole in the Grand Canyon, or we'd be up the proverbial stink creek without a paddle. You do have more bandages, don't you, Virginia?"

"In the medicine cabinet." Virginia winced as the last of the gauze was peeled away.

Steadying herself on the vanity, she looked in the mirror. Her left breast had a chunk the size of a silver dollar carved out of it. Virginia turned quickly away from the mirror, unable to bear the sight of her disfigurement.

"It's hideous. Cover it back up." She sank onto the toilet seat.

"It's not hideous. It's hardly even noticeable."

"Only the blind wouldn't notice. I'm lopsided. My clothes won't fit. Even my bras won't fit."

"It will eventually fill back in. That's what the doctor said, Virginia."

Virginia didn't hear her; she was too busy tasting the salt of her own tears.

"Make him go away, Jane."

Jane didn't have to ask who. Silently she rebound Virginia's breast.

"I don't want to see him again. I *can't* see him again. Ever."

Virginia leaned on Jane and allowed herself to be helped back into bed as if she were an invalid. Jane pulled the covers over her, then quietly removed the food.

"Sleep, Virginia. Everything will look different in the morning. You'll see."

"Do you think all this will go away overnight? Do you think I'm going to wake up and have a whole breast?"

Jane extinguished all the lights except a small lamp inside the bathroom door before she came back to the bed.

"The thing that matters most is that you have a whole mind and a whole personality and a whole spirit, Virginia."

She could barely hear Jane moving across the room, barely see her as she got blankets from the closet shelf and spread them on the chaise longue. The room was so quiet, Virginia could hear the faint chimes of the grandfather clock downstairs. Outside the moon shone on Bolton's cottage, the windows now dark. Downstairs Candace would be trying to get a good night's sleep before her drive back to college.

Virginia forced herself not to think about her body,

about what had been done to it and what might be happening to it even as she slept.

"Jane . . ."

"Hmmm?"

"I don't know what I would do without you."

"You don't have to find out. Go to sleep, Virginia."

"Okay. I'll try."

NINETEEN

Bolton sat on a bar stool in Virginia's kitchen, drinking coffee, while Jane added a glass of orange juice to the breakfast tray she was preparing.

"I'll take that upstairs," he said.

"I'm sorry. She won't see you, Bolton."

"Why? Yesterday everything seemed to be all right. What happened to change her mind?"

"She saw the scar on her breast."

"That's all? Does she think that matters to me?"

"Yes, she thinks that. More important, it matters to her. Bolton, do you have any idea the role a woman's breasts play in her self-image? Not only are they symbols of nurturing, but they are vital to our feelings of sensuality and desirability. Right now, Virginia feels undesirable and disfigured. Besides that, she's worried about having cancer, and she's bound and determined to protect you from that."

He tore a piece of paper off the notepad on the bar

and began to write. Curious, Jane tried to read over his shoulder.

"All of you writers are just alike. Nobody can read your handwriting."

Bolton folded the paper in half and handed it to Jane.

"Please give this to Virginia."

"What is it?"

"A message."

"Okay, I get the picture. It's none of my business." She stuffed it into her pocket, picked up the tray, and started toward the door. "I'll try to resist the temptation to read it before I give it to her."

"Thanks, Jane."

"You bet."

Virginia was standing beside the window when Jane went into her bedroom. In the distance her Arabians raced across the pasture, their manes and tails streaming like white flags.

"I wish I could ride," she said. "There's something wonderfully liberating about racing along with the wind in my hair and the sun on my face and nothing around me except earth and sky and trees." She sat in the chair beside the window and gazed wistfully at Jane.

"I don't feel in control of my life anymore. When I'm on my horse, nothing else seems to matter; everything falls into its proper place. Does that make any sense, Jane?"

"You always make sense, Virginia. You're the most sensible person I know. Sometimes I wonder if you're too sensible."

"What do you mean? Too sensible?"

Indiscreet

Jane reached into her pocket and pulled out the note. "Here, read this first." She handed Virginia the note. "From Bolton."

Virginia refolded the note and held it in her lap.

"What's the use of reading it? A note won't change a thing."

"That's what I mean." Jane squatted beside her chair and covered Virginia's hands with hers. "I know I said some things that made you think that I think a match between you and Bolton would be about the worst disaster since Hurricane Camille tore through the Gulf Coast, but I had no right to make that kind of judgment. Nor does anybody else. Forget everything and everybody. You've always been intrepid, Virginia. My land, look how far you've come! Be intrepid again and reach out for what you want."

"What I want would not be fair to Bolton."

"Why don't you let him be the judge of that?"

Slowly Virginia unfolded the note. Bolton's handwriting was exactly what she had expected, big and bold with straight, decisive lines.

"Virginia," he had written. "You are my life, my love, and nothing else matters. NOTHING! Each moment we are not together is a waste. Together we are a miracle; apart we are two lonely people filled with regret. Marry me, Virginia. Let's not waste our tomorrows."

She read the note twice before she refolded it and put it in the top drawer of her bedside table.

"Well . . . What did he say?"

"Nothing that would convince me to change my mind." Virginia hastily scribbled on a notepad, then tore the page off and handed it to Jane. "Will you take him this?"

"Shoot, I fancied myself as Cupid when all along I was nothing but the pony express." At Virginia's withering look, Jane threw up her hands. "All right, all right. I'll take it."

Bolton was waiting for her at the bottom of the stairs.

"What did she say?"

"Here." Jane handed him the note. "This is what she said."

Virginia's reply was brief: "Bolton, for me tomorrow may never come. I can't and I *won't* saddle you with my problems."

Bolton was so still that Jane thought he had forgotten she was there.

"Will there be a reply?"

"No. No reply." He started toward the door, then remembered his manners. "Thanks, Jane."

"Wait. Where are you going? You're not giving up, are you?"

"Never." He smiled at her. "There's an old Apache saying that wisdom comes to us in dreams."

Virginia stood at her window and watched Bolton go down the path to the cottage, then enter. She could see movement behind the windows. What was he doing? Packing?

She heard Jane enter the room, but Virginia didn't

Indiscreet

turn around; she *couldn't* turn around, not as long as there was a chance to catch a glimpse of Bolton.

"What did he say?" she asked.

"Just that."

"What?"

"The same thing you just said, except that he said, 'What did *she* say?'"

"Oh . . . Is there a note?"

"No. No note."

Virginia wadded the curtain in her hand, her eyes riveted on the guest cottage. The curtains were open to let in the autumn sunlight, and through the French doors she could see him at the desk, using the telephone. Who was he calling?

"Did he say *anything*?"

"Some old Indian wisdom about Apaches coming with dreams."

"What?"

"Or maybe it was dreams coming with Apaches."

"Good grief. That doesn't sound like Bolton."

"That's what I say. Good grief." Jane puttered around the room, picking up every movable object. "Do you want to play checkers, Virginia?"

"No. I want you to go home and get some rest."

"You haven't heard from Dr. Mason."

"I'm not likely to hear today, and I'm not planning to fall apart today, either." She caught her friend's hand. "Look, Jane. I feel better this morning, stronger. I thought I might even go downstairs and work at the computer awhile. Anything to keep my mind off myself while I wait to hear from the doctor."

"If you think I'm leaving you till he calls, you've got another think coming." Jane set up the checkerboard. "Do you want black or red?"

"Black. It fits my mood."

Jane set up the board. "And don't cheat. You always cheat."

"I do not. You say that because I always win."

Jane made her first move. "What do you reckon he meant about Apaches coming with dreams?"

Virginia shrugged her shoulders, then made her move. But her mind was not on the game; it was on an incredibly passionate Apache who had come to her bearing a dream, not once, not twice, but three times. Was she crazy to keep spitting in the eye of fate?

She never even noticed when Jane jumped her and swept her checker off the board.

TWENTY

At midafternoon Bolton left on some mysterious errand and didn't return until long after dark. If Jane had been awake, Virginia would have discussed his whereabouts with her, but Jane was stretched out on the chaise longue snoring. Exhausted.

Virginia watched as Bolton rounded the curve in the pathway that led to the cottage. He paused at the door and gazed upward toward the window where she stood. The moon slanted across his face so that she could see each feature distinctly, the high cheekbones, the sensual mouth, the solid jaw, the piercing blue eyes. Virginia's heart kicked into double time, and she pressed her hand over the front of her gown.

His mouth moved, and though she couldn't hear the words she knew exactly what he was saying. "I love you."

"Don't," she whispered. "Oh, please, don't."

For an instance his face was illuminated by one of his quicksilver smiles, and then he was gone, gliding through the door and into the cottage like one of the big, graceful wildcats she had seen on his mountain.

A terrible sense of loss weighed Virginia down and sapped all her energy. She dragged herself to the bathroom. When she caught sight of herself in the mirror, she flinched. The bandage covering her breast was a reminder of what lay underneath.

Virginia jerked a towel off the rack and draped it over the mirror, shutting out the hateful image. The tightening in her throat signaled a gathering of tears. She felt totally helpless, even more helpless than she had when Roger left her.

Suddenly Virginia remembered those days, days of wondering how she could raise her child and pay her bills alone, days of wondering where her next bit of strength would come from, her next bit of hope.

Intrepid, Jane had called her. And by George, she had been. She *was*.

She marched to the mirror, tore the towel off, and stared at herself. There was nothing wrong with the outside of her that a good shampoo and a good bath wouldn't fix. As for the inside . . . she would cross that bridge when she came to it. And if cancer was waiting for her on the other side, she would fight a battle the likes of which had never been fought.

"You're not going to beat Virginia Haven," she said. "Don't even try."

Her chin held high and her step firm, she made her way to bed and was asleep almost before her head hit the pillow. She didn't stir until the phone woke her the next morning.

"Virginia, this is Dr. Mason . . ."

She gripped the receiver so hard, her knuckles turned white.

"I didn't expect to hear from you so soon."

"I didn't expect to call you so soon. The test results are in."

Virginia drew a deep breath. There would be no tears and no trembling for her today, just a good firm resolve that she would face whatever lay ahead with grace and courage and a tenacious will to win.

"What is it . . . who is it . . ." Jane sat up, her eyes still heavy with sleep and her hair poufed like a giant Christmas bow that had been battered about.

"Shhh . . . it's Dr. Mason. . . ." Virginia held the receiver close to her ear, hardly daring to breathe. "What was that? . . . I see . . . You're sure? . . . Yes, so am I . . . Thank you, Dr. Mason."

Virginia's legs wouldn't hold her. She sank onto the edge of the bed.

"I can't believe it. I just can't believe it," she said.

"What?" Jane raced across the room, her sheet tangled in her pajama buttons and dragging along behind her. "What can't you believe?" Virginia merely stared at her. "I'm going to have a heart attack . . . Virginia, was it that bad?"

"It was amazing, a miracle. That's what Dr. Mason called it, a miracle."

"Then it's not cancer?"

"It's not cancer."

The two friends stared at each other, then they began to laugh and cry at the same time. Jane did a victory dance around the room, whooping and hollering, then threw herself onto the bed.

"Tell all. What did he say?"

"Because of the X rays from the mammogram and the location, Dr. Mason was certain it was cancer. So was the pathologist. When he saw the mass during surgery, he was furious that I had refused to sign so that they could remove my breast."

"That's why Dr. Mason wouldn't tell us what the pathologist had thought."

"Exactly . . . Then the result of the frozen section came in." Virginia beamed. "It's a miracle, Jane."

Jane went into the bathroom to blow her nose and came back trailing toilet paper. "Shoot, it looks like I'm on a crying jag and fixing to wallow in it all day."

"Go ahead and wallow; you've earned the right."

"What about you? What are you going to do?"

"Laugh, dance, sing, bathe, shampoo. Not necessarily in that order." But there was one thing above all others that she had to do. "I want to see Bolton. I need to see Bolton."

She picked up the receiver and dialed the cottage. The phone rang and rang.

"I must have dialed the wrong number." She dialed again and waited, listening to the insistent rings in a cottage that obviously was not occupied.

"I guess he had second thoughts." Quietly Virginia replaced the receiver. "Who can blame him?"

"Hey, chin up, pal. This is not the end, you know."

"No, it's not." Smiling, Virginia slipped on her robe. "As a matter of fact, it's just the beginning."

"You're darned right."

"Jane . . . I don't know what I would do without you."

"The same right back at you." Jane sniffled into a wad of toilet paper. "Let me get out of here before I start again."

After Jane left, Virginia called Candace, then shut herself into the bathroom for a major overhaul. In bubbles up to her bandage she fancied that she heard music, a melody that reminded her of mountains alive with birdsong and newly greening trees and spring flowers.

She toweled her hair dry, spritzed herself with perfume that smelled like flowers in the summer sun, then put on her pink robe and shoved open the door.

"Hello, Virginia."

Bolton stood beside the window smiling. The music was distinct now, Leonard Bernstein playing Copland's "Appalachian Spring." The music filled her soul, and the man filled her vision, tall, bronzed, incredibly gorgeous, his eyes flashing blue fire. For a moment Virginia was speechless, lost in the absolute beauty of the man who had shared her bed and claimed her heart.

"You brought the music," she said.

"Yes. I brought the music."

Bolton crossed the room in three long strides. Only when he was standing in front of her did she notice what he had in his hand, an Indian blanket, brilliantly hued in all the colors of the rainbow.

"I'm glad you're wearing the pink robe," he said, draping his blanket around her shoulders. Then tenderly he lifted her into his arms. "It's perfect."

"For what?"

"For making a fresh start."

As he left the room and headed down the stairs, the Bernstein orchestra segued into Copland's lusty, dashing "Fanfare for the Common Man."

"Where are you taking me?"

"On a journey that has no end."

Music drifted around them as Bolton strode boldly through her living room, across the foyer, and out the front door. One of her white Arabians was just beyond the front porch, bridled and covered with another Apache blanket.

Virginia didn't even consider protesting as Bolton carefully lifted her onto the stallion and mounted in front of her. Her curiosity was aroused, and she had to find out what he was up to. But more than that, she was filled with a sense of the inevitable, of being swept along on a wave that she could no more control than she could dictate the tides of the ocean.

"Hold on tight, Virginia. Don't let go."

"I won't." She wrapped her arms around Bolton's waist and leaned her head against his back. "I don't want to ever let go," she whispered, but her words were lost in the wind and the pounding of hooves.

Overhead the sky was as blue as a robin's egg, and spread out around her was her land, its hills and meadows and forests and lakes polished by the sun and strewn with the colors of autumn. Exhilaration filled Virginia. The land was solid and enduring, a continual source of strength.

What did it matter the curves life threw her as long

as she had the land? What did it matter where life took her as long as she had Bolton?

They passed the barn and the paddocks, rounded the lake and topped a hill, and there in the distance was Bolton's tepee, rising almost as tall as the trees around it.

"How in the world . . ."

"Callie dismantled it and shipped it express." He drew the Arabian to a stop and dismounted, handling Virginia as carefully as if she were breakable. "We didn't finish what we started, and since you can't go back to the mountain for a while, I brought the mountain to you."

"You're a remarkable man."

"So are you—a remarkable woman."

He opened the blanket and stepped into its protective folds, drawing it around their shoulders so that they stood thigh to thigh, chest to chest, heart to heart.

"I love you, Virginia Haven. I've loved you since the moment I saw you riding like an Apache on your white stallion, your hair the color of corn silk and your skin blooming as if roses were trapped underneath."

The nearness of him set her aflame, and she pressed closer, reveling in the heat of his body and the size of his arousal.

"I covered you with my blanket and made you mine. I filled you with my seed and claimed you forever. The branches of my heart are entangled with yours, and nothing can ever tear us apart."

He claimed her with a kiss so sweet, so tender that she would have sworn she heard angels singing. Then he picked her up and carried her inside his tepee.

"Bolton . . . there's something I have to tell you. Something very important."

"Nothing is important now except this . . ." He spread the blanket on the floor of his tepee and lay down with Virginia cradled in his arms. Bending over her, he fanned out her fair hair so that it made a halo around her face. Then he kissed the silky strands.

Virginia forgot everything except her incredibly sexy Apache warrior and the sensations he evoked. He kissed her eyebrows, her nose, her cheeks. He lingered over her lips, nibbling and tasting, probing and devouring.

"Bolton . . . I need you." She wrapped her arms tightly around him. "Don't stop . . . please don't stop."

"Never, my love, never."

He moved his attentions downward, caressing her neck with lips and hands. Only when he caught the sash of her robe did she remember her bandages . . . and the damage they hid.

She caught the neck of her robe and held it tightly closed. He covered her hands with his.

"I'm scarred, Bolton."

"The only scars that matter are the ones that damage the heart and the soul. You are whole, Virginia."

Suddenly Virginia realized that there would be no halfway measures with this man. If she loved him, she would have to give herself completely to him, scars and all.

She released her hold, and Bolton spread her robe open. He bent to her right breast and suckled deeply, then he touched the bandage that covered her left. Ten-

Indiscreet

derly, almost reverently he kissed the bandage that hid her.

She buried her fingers in his hair and pulled him close. Such love filled her that she thought she might shatter into a thousand shining pieces, each one as brilliant as a star.

"Do you love me, Virginia?" Bolton lifted his head and looked down at her.

"Yes, Bolton. Oh, yes." He claimed her lips, and they kissed until desire flamed so hot, it could no longer be denied. "I love you, I love you," she said as he parted her thighs and slid home.

And she knew beyond a shadow of a doubt that what she had found with Bolton Gray Wolf was true love, that their meeting was no accident but destiny, that their future had been decreed by a power far wiser than she. All her reasons for refusing him vanished like chafe before a strong wind, and Virginia was free, free to give and to receive a passion that had no bounds, free to love and to be loved as only the unencumbered can.

Mindful of her recent surgery, Bolton was gentle with her, and so tender that she felt as if she were floating high above the earth, borne upward on the wings of eagles. Inside the tepee they soared, while outside the sun rose high in the sky and the brisk autumn winds died down to a soft murmur.

She opened herself to him in a way she never had, and when he spilled his seed, he cried out his wonder in the language she understood with her heart. Afterward he held her close, wrapped in her pink robe and the edge of his blanket.

"You have my heart, Virginia. Say you'll take my name, as well."

The generosity and complete faith of his offer astounded Virginia.

"You would marry me without knowing whether I have cancer? Without knowing whether I have one breast or two?"

"One of the most beautiful creatures of legend has only one horn."

"The unicorn?"

"Yes, the unicorn." Bolton stroked her hair. "A creature gifted with powers of magic. Only a fool would throw away magic."

Virginia smiled. "Is that an answer?"

"That's my answer."

"My left breast is scarred but otherwise intact, and I don't have cancer. Dr. Mason calls it a miracle."

"The Father Creator heard my prayers."

Bolton kissed her brow, then propped on his elbow so he could see the face that was more precious to him than any other face in the world. Bolton captured her with a riveting blue gaze and slowly extended his right hand.

There was no hesitation in Virginia now, only a beautiful certainty. She placed her hand in his, smiling.

"Yes, Virginia, it's a miracle, but the greatest miracle of all is love."

EPILOGUE

Virginia never tired of watching the sunset in the mountains. She swiveled her chair toward the window so she could see the sky change from blue to rose and gold then fade to a dusky pink that gave way to deep purple. Only when the shadows lay across the mountains did she turn back to her computer.

She typed the last word of the last sentence in the last chapter of her latest novel, and then she scrolled to another page to type the dedication.

"To my beloved, whose love defines my minutes, my hours, my days, my years."

As soon as Bolton entered the room, all her attention was focused on him. His cameras were slung around his neck, and his dog Bear followed at his heels. He wrapped his arms around her from behind the chair and rested his chin on her hair as he read over her shoulder.

"Is this *beloved* someone I should know about?" he said, teasing her.

"Maybe. He stole my heart two years ago, and I've dedicated every one of my novels to him."

"He's important to you, is he?"

"He's my life, my love, my heart."

Laughing, he picked her up and carried her outside.

"What do you see?" he asked.

"A barn. Horses. Trees. Pasture. A mountain."

"What else?"

"You." She ruffled his hair and kissed his lips.

"What else?"

She wrinkled her brow then glanced upward. "A sliver of a moon and the first pale stars of evening."

"Anything else?"

"No . . ."

"You're sure?"

"Bolton . . . what is all this mystery?"

He set her on her feet and draped his left arm over her shoulder. Then with his right he pointed to the clearing beyond the first ridge of the mountains.

"I see a house, one large enough for at least a dozen people. I see a basketball court and a swimming pool surrounded by a running track. I see flower gardens and pets and a kind older couple with enough love in their hearts to spare for battered and abused kids." He paused, smiling down at her. "I see a place called Safe Haven."

He grabbed her hand and raced back toward their house. Inside, he pulled a blueprint out of his back pocket and spread it across the coffee table. *Safe Haven* was printed in large blue letters at the top, and beneath was the architect's concept of a spacious home that would shelter the children society forgot, teenagers in trouble at home, children whose parents had no jobs and no way to care for them, children battered and bruised with no place to go.

"Just think," Bolton said. "We can see those kids two or three times a week, teach them to play ball, to fish, to read good books, to care for the environment, to love and appreciate nature. What do you think, Virginia?"

She cupped his face, pulled him close, and kissed him.

"I think the same thing I thought when I first met you. You are remarkable, and I am the luckiest person in the world."

"The same right back at you, Mrs. Gray Wolf."

THE EDITORS' CORNER

What do a cowboy, a straitlaced professor, a federal agent, and a wildlife photographer have in common? They're the sizzling men you'll meet in next month's LOVESWEPT lineup, and they're uniting with wonderful heroines for irresistible tales of passion and romance. Packed with emotion, these terrific stories are guaranteed to keep you enthralled. Enjoy!

Longtime romance favorite Karen Leabo begins the glorious BRIDES OF DESTINY series with **CALLIE'S COWBOY**, LOVESWEPT #806, a story of poignant magic, tender promises, and revealing truths. Sam Sanger had always planned to share his ranch and his future with Callie Calloway, but even in high school he understood that loving this woman might mean letting her go! When a fortune-teller hinted that her fate lay with Sam, Callie ran—afraid a life with Sam would mean sacrificing her dreams. Now, ten years later, she stops running long enough to wonder if Sam is the destiny she most desires. Displaying the style that has made her a #1 bestselling author, Karen Leabo explores the deep longings that lead us to love.

Warming hearts and tickling funny bones from start to finish, award-winner Jennifer Crusie creates her own fairy tale of love in **THE CINDERELLA DEAL**, LOVESWEPT #807. Linc Blaise needs the perfect fiancée to win his dream job, but finding a woman who'll be convincing in the charade seems impossible—until he hears Daisy Flattery charm her way out of a sticky situation! The bedazzling storyteller knows it'll be a snap playing a prim and proper lady to Linc's serious professor, but the pretense turns into a risky temptation when she discovers the vulnerable side Linc tries so hard to hide. Jennifer Crusie debuts in LOVESWEPT with an utterly charming story of opposites attracting.

Acclaimed author Laura Taylor provides a **SLIGHTLY SCANDALOUS** scenario for her memorable hero and heroine in her newest LOVESWEPT, #808. Trapped with a rugged stranger when a sudden storm stops an elevator between floors, Claire Duncan is shocked to feel the undeniable heat of attraction! In Tate Richmond she senses strength shadowed by a loneliness that echoes her own unspoken need. Vowing to explore the hunger that sparks between them, forced by unusual circumstances to resort to clandestine meetings, Tate draws her to him with tender ferocity. He has always placed honor above desire, kept himself safe in a world of constant peril, but once he's trusted his destiny to a woman of mystery, he can't live without her touch.

Laura Taylor packs quite a punch with this exquisite romance!

RaeAnne Thayne sets the mood with reckless passion and fierce destiny in **WILD STREAK,** LOVESWEPT #809. Keen Malone can't believe his ears when Meg O'Neill turns him down for a loan! Determined to make the cool beauty understand that his wildlife center is the mountain's only hope, he persuades her to tour the site. Meg can't deny the lush beauty of the land he loves, but how long can she fight the wild longing to run into his arms? RaeAnne Thayne creates a swirl of undeniable attraction in this classic romance of two strangers who discover they share the same fierce desire.

Happy reading!

With warmest wishes,

Beth de Guzman   Shauna Summers

Senior Editor   Editor

P.S. Watch for these Bantam women's fiction titles coming in October. Praised by Amanda Quick as "an exciting find for romance readers everywhere," Elizabeth Elliott dazzles with **BETROTHED,** the much anticipated sequel to her debut novel, THE WARLORD. When Guy of Montague finds himself trapped in an engagement to Claudia, Baron Lonsdale's beautiful niece, his only thought is escape. But when she comes to his rescue, with the condition that he take her with him, he finds himself under her spell, willing to risk everything—even his life—to capture her heart. And don't miss **TAME THE WILD WIND** by Rosanne Bittner, the mistress of romantic frontier fiction. Half-breed Gabe Beaumont rides with a renegade Sioux band until a raid on a Wyoming stage post unites him with Faith Kelley. Together they will face their destinies and fight for their love against the shadows of their own wild hearts.

Be sure to see next month's LOVESWEPTs for a preview of these exceptional novels. And immediately following this page, preview the Bantam women's fiction titles on sale *now*!

Don't miss these extraordinary books
by your favorite Bantam authors

On sale in August:

AMANDA
by Kay Hooper

THE MARSHAL AND THE HEIRESS
by Patricia Potter

TEXAS LOVER
by Adrienne deWolfe

"Amanda seethes and sizzles. A fast-paced atmospheric tale that vibrates with tension, passion, and mystery."—Catherine Coulter

AMANDA

from bestselling author
Kay Hooper
now available in paperback

When a missing heiress to a vast fortune suddenly reappears, there's good reason for suspicion. After all, others before her had claimed to be Amanda Daulton; is this poised woman the genuine article or another impostor hoping to cash in? Unlike the family patriarch, others at the Southern mansion called Glory are not so easily swayed by Amanda's claim. They have too much at stake—enough, perhaps, to commit murder. . . .

July, 1975

Thunder rolled and boomed, echoing the way it did when a storm came over the mountains on a hot night, and the wind-driven rain lashed the trees and furiously pelted the windowpanes of the big house. The nine-year-old girl shivered, her cotton nightgown soaked and clinging to her, and her slight body was stiff as she stood in the center of the dark bedroom.

"Mama—"

"Shhhh! Don't, baby, don't make any noise. Just stand there, very still, and wait for me."

They called her baby often, her mother, her father, because she'd been so difficult to conceive and was so cherished once they had her. So beloved. That was why they had named her Amanda, her father had explained, lifting her up to ride upon his broad shoulders, because she was so perfect and so worthy of their love.

She didn't feel perfect now. She felt cold and emptied out and dreadfully afraid. And the sound of her mother's voice, so thin and desperate, frightened Amanda even more. The bottom had fallen out of her world so suddenly that she was still numbly bewildered and broken, and her big gray eyes followed her mother with the piteous dread of one who had lost everything except a last fragile, unspeakably precious tie to what had been.

Whispering between rumbles of thunder, she asked, "Mama, where will we go?"

"Away, far away, baby." The only illumination in the bedroom was provided by angry nature as lightning split the stormy sky outside, and Christine Daulton used the flashes to guide her in stuffing clothes into an old canvas duffel bag. She dared not turn on any lights, and the need to hurry was so fierce it nearly strangled her.

She hadn't room for them, but she pushed her journals into the bag as well because she had to have *something* of this place to take with her, and something of her life with Brian. *Oh, dear God, Brian* . . . She raked a handful of jewelry from the box on the dresser, tasting blood because she was biting her bottom lip to keep herself from screaming. There was no time, no time, she had to get Amanda away from here.

"Wait here," she told her daughter.

"No! Mama, please—"

"Shhhh! All right, Amanda, come with me—but you have to be quiet." Moments later, down the hall in her daughter's room, Christine fumbled for more clothing and thrust it into the bulging bag. She helped the silent, trembling girl into dry clothing, faded jeans and a tee shirt. "Shoes?"

Amanda found a pair of dirty sneakers and shoved her feet into them. Her mother grasped her hand and led her from the room, both of them consciously tiptoeing. Then, at the head of the stairs, Amanda suddenly let out a moan of anguish and tried to pull her hand free. "Oh, I *can't*—"

"Shhhh," Christine warned urgently. "Amanda—"

Even whispering, Amanda's voice held a desperate intensity. "Mama, please, Mama, I have to get something—I can't leave it here, please, Mama—it'll only take a second—"

She had no idea what could be so precious to her daughter, but Christine wasn't about to drag her down the stairs in this state of wild agitation. The child was already in shock, a breath away from absolute hysteria. "All right, but hurry. And *be quiet.*"

As swift and silent as a shadow, Amanda darted back down the hallway and vanished into her bedroom. She reappeared less than a minute later, shoving something into the front pocket of her jeans. Christine didn't pause to find out what was so important that Amanda couldn't bear to leave it behind; she simply grabbed her daughter's free hand and continued down the stairs.

The grandfather clock on the landing whirred and bonged a moment before they reached it, announcing in sonorous tones that it was two A.M. The sound was too familiar to startle either of them, and they hurried on without pause. The front door was still open, as they'd left it, and Christine didn't bother to pull it shut behind them as they went through to the wide porch.

The wind had blown rain halfway over the porch to the door, and Amanda dimly heard her shoes squeak on the wet stone. Then she ducked her head against the rain and stuck close to her mother as they raced for the car parked several yards away. By the time she was sitting in the front seat watching her mother fumble with the keys, Amanda was soaked again and shivering, despite a temperature in the seventies.

The car's engine coughed to life, and its headlights stabbed through the darkness and sheeting rain to illuminate the graveled driveway. Amanda turned her head to the side as the car jolted toward the paved road, and she caught her breath when she saw a light bobbing far away between the house and the stables, as if someone was running with a flashlight. Running toward the car that, even then, turned onto the paved road and picked up speed as it left the house behind.

Quickly, Amanda turned her gaze forward again, rubbing her cold hands together, swallowing hard as sickness rose in her aching throat. "Mama? We can't come back, can we? We can't ever come back?"

The tears running down her ashen cheeks almost but not quite blinding her, Christine Daulton replied, "No, Amanda. We can't ever come back."

"One of the romance genre's finest talents."
—Romantic Times

From
Patricia Potter
bestselling author of *DIABLO*
comes

THE MARSHAL AND THE HEIRESS

When U.S. Marshal Ben Masters became Sarah Ann's guardian, he didn't know she was the lost heir to a Scottish estate—or that her life would soon be in danger. Now, instead of hunting down a gun-toting outlaw, he faces an aristocratic household bitterly divided by ambition. And not even falling in love with Sarah Ann's beautiful young aunt could keep her from being a suspect in Ben's eyes.

How do you tell a four-year-old girl that her mother is dead?

U.S. Marshal Ben Masters worried over the question as he stood on the porch of Mrs. Henrietta Culworthy's small house. Then, squaring his shoulders, he knocked. He wished he really believed he was doing the right thing. What in God's name did a man like him, a man who'd lived with guns and violence for the past eight years, have to offer an orphaned child?

Mary May believed in you. The thought raked through his heart. He felt partially responsible for her death. He had stirred a pot without considering the consequences. In bringing an end to an infamous outlaw hideout, he had been oblivious to those caught in the cross fire. The fact that Mary May had been involved with the outlaws didn't assuage his conscience.

Sarah. Promise you'll take care of Sarah. He would never forget Mary May's last faltering words.

Ben rapped again on the door of the house. Mrs. Culworthy should be expecting him. She had been looking after Sarah Ann for the past three years, but now she had to return east to care for a brother. She had already postponed her trip once, agreeing to wait until Ben had wiped out the last remnants of an outlaw band and fulfilled a promise to the former renegade named Diablo.

The door opened. Mrs. Culworthy's wrinkled face appeared, sagging slightly with relief. Had she worried that he would not return? He sure as hell had thought about it. He'd thought about a lot of things, like where he might find another suitable home for Sarah Ann. But then he would never be sure she was being raised properly. By God, he owed Mary May.

"Sarah Ann?" he asked Mrs. Culworthy.

"In her room." The woman eyed him hopefully. "You *are* going to take her."

He nodded.

"What about your job?"

"I'm resigning. I used to be a lawyer. Thought I would hang up my shingle in Denver."

A smile spread across Mrs. Culworthy's face. "Thank heaven for you. I love that little girl. I would take her if I could, but—"

"I know you would," he said gently. "But she'll be safe with me." He hoped that was true. He hesitated. "She doesn't know yet, does she? About her mother?"

Mrs. Culworthy shook her head.

Just then, a small head adorned with reddish curls

and green eyes peered around the door. Excitement lit the gamin face. "Mama's here!"

Pain thrust through Ben. Of course, Sarah Ann would think her mother had arrived. Mary May had been here with him just a few weeks ago.

"Uncle Ben," the child said, "where's Mama?"

He wished Mrs. Culworthy had already told her. He was sick of being the bearer of bad news, and never more so than now.

He dropped to one knee and held out a hand to the little girl. "She's gone to heaven," Ben said.

She approached slowly, her face wrinkling in puzzlement; then she looked questioningly at Mrs. Culworthy. The woman dissolved into tears. Ben didn't know whether Sarah Ann understood what was being said, but she obviously sensed that something was very wrong. The smile disappeared and her underlip started to quiver.

Ben's heart quaked. He had guarded that battered part of him these past years, but there were no defenses high enough, or thick enough, to withstand a child's tears.

He held out his arms, not sure Sarah Ann knew him well enough to accept his comfort. But she walked into his embrace, and he hugged her, stiffly at first. Unsure. But then her need overtook his uncertainty, and his grip tightened.

"You asked me once if I were your papa," he said. "Would you like me to be?"

Sarah Ann looked up at him. "Isn't Mama coming back?"

He shook his head. "She can't, but she loved you so much she asked me to take care of you. If that's all right with you?"

Sarah Ann turned to Mrs. Culworthy. "I want to stay with you, Cully."

"You can't, Pumpkin," Mrs. Culworthy said tenderly. "I have to go east, but Mr. Masters will take good care of you. Your mother thought so, too."

"Where is heaven? Can't I go, too?"

"Someday," Ben said slowly. "And she'll be waiting for you, but right now I need you. I need someone to take care of me, too, and your mama thought we could take care of each other."

It was true, he suddenly realized. He did need someone to love. His life had been empty for so long.

Sarah Ann probably had much to offer him.

But what did he have to offer her?

Sarah Ann put her hand to his cheek. The tiny fingers were incredibly soft—softer than anything he'd ever felt—and gentle. She had lost everything, yet she was comforting him.

He hugged her close for a moment, and then he stood. Sarah Ann's hand crept into his. Trustingly. And Ben knew he would die before ever letting anything bad happen to her again.

"Adrienne deWolfe writes with power and passion."—*New York Times* bestselling author Arnette Lamb

TEXAS LOVER

by

Adrienne deWolfe

author of *TEXAS OUTLAW*

To Texas Ranger Wes Rawlins, settling a property dispute should be no trickier than peeling potatoes—even if it does involve a sheriff's cousin and a headstrong schoolmarm on opposite camps. But Wes quickly learns there's more to the matter than meets the eye. The only way to get at the truth is from the inside. So posing as a carpenter, the lawman uncovers more than he bargains for in a feisty beauty and her house full of orphans.

"Sons of thunder."

Rorie rarely resorted to such unladylike outbursts, but the strain of her predicament was wearing on her. She had privately conceded she could not face Hannibal Dukker with the same laughable lack of shooting skill she had displayed for Wes Rawlins. So, swallowing her great distaste for guns—and the people who solved their problems with them—she had forced herself to ride out to the woods early, before the children arrived for their lessons, to practice her marksmanship.

It was a good thing she had done so.

She had just fired her sixth round, her *sixth round*, for heaven's sake, and that abominable whiskey bottle still sat untouched on the top of her barrel. If she had been a fanciful woman—which she most assuredly was not—she might have imagined that impudent vessel was trying to provoke her. Why, it hadn't rattled once when her bullets whizzed by. And the long rays of morning sun had fired it a bright and frolicsome green. If there was one thing she couldn't abide, it was a frolicsome whiskey bottle.

Her mouth set in a grim line, she fished in the pocket of her pinafore for more bullets.

Thus occupied, Rorie didn't immediately notice the tremor of the earth beneath her boots. She didn't ascribe anything unusual to her nag's snorting or the way Daisy stomped her hoof and tossed her head. The beast was chronically fractious.

Soon, though, Rorie detected the sound of thrashing, as if a powerful animal were breaking through the brush around the clearing. Her heart quickened, but she tried to remain calm. After all, bears were hardly as brutish as their hunters liked to tell. And any other wild animal with sense would turn tail and run once it got wind of her human scent—not to mention a whiff of her gunpowder.

Still, it might be wise to start reloading. . . .

A bloodcurdling whoop shook her hands. She couldn't line up a single bullet with its chamber. She thought to run, but there was nowhere to hide, and Daisy was snapping too viciously to mount.

Suddenly the sun winked out of sight. A horse, a *mammoth* horse with fiery eyes and steaming nostrils, sailed toward her over the barrel. She tried to scream, but it lodged in her throat as an "eek." All she could do was stand there, jaw hanging, knees knocking, and remember the unfortunate schoolmaster, Ichabod Crane.

Only her horseman had a head.

A red head, to be exact. And he carried it above his shoulders, rather than tucked under his arm.

"God a'mighty! Miss Aurora!"

The rider reined in so hard that his gelding reared, shrilling in indignation. Her revolver slid from her fingers. She saw a peacemaker in the rider's fist, and she thought again about running.

"It's me, ma'am. Wes Rawlins," he called, then cursed as his horse wheeled and pawed.

She blinked uncertainly, still poised to flee. He didn't look like the dusty longrider who'd drunk from her well the previous afternoon. His hair was sleek and short, and his cleft chin was bare of all but morning stubble. Although he did still wear the mustache, it was the gunbelt that gave him away. She recognized the double holsters before she recognized his strong, sculpted features.

He managed to subdue his horse before it could bolt back through the trees. "Are you all right, ma'am?" He hastily dismounted, releasing his reins to ground-hitch the gelding. "Uh-oh." He peered into her face. "You aren't gonna faint or anything, are you?"

She snapped erect, mortified by the very suggestion. "Certainly not. I've never been sick a day in my life. And swooning is for invalids."

"Sissies, too," he agreed solemnly.

He ran an appreciative gaze over her hastily piled hair and down her crisply pressed pinafore to her mud-spattered boots. She felt the blood surge to her cheeks. Masking her discomfort, she planted both fists on her hips.

"*Mister* Rawlins. What on earth is the matter with you, tearing around the countryside like that? You frightened the devil out of my horse!"

"I'm real sorry, ma'am. I never meant to give

your, er, *horse* such a fright. But you see, I heard gunshots. And since there's nothing out this way except the Boudreau homestead, I thought you might be having trouble."

"Trouble?" She felt her heart flutter. Had he heard something of Dukker's intentions?

"Well, sure. Yesterday, the way you had those children running for cover, I thought you might be expecting some." He folded his arms across his chest. "Are you?"

The directness of his question—and his gaze—was unsettling. He no longer reminded her of a lion. Today he was a fox, slick and clever, with a dash of sly charm thrown in to confuse her. She hastily bolstered her defenses.

"Did it ever occur to you, Mr. Rawlins, that Shae might be out here shooting rabbits?"

"Nope. Never thought I'd find you here, either. Not that I mind, ma'am. Not one bit. You see, I'm the type who likes surprises. Especially pleasant ones."

She felt her face grow warmer. She wasn't used to flattery. Her husband had been too preoccupied with self-pity to spare many kind words for her in the last two years of their marriage.

"Well," she said, "I never expected to see you out here either, Mr. Rawlins."

"Call me Wes."

She forced herself to ignore his winsome smile. "In truth, sir, I never thought to see you again."

"Why's that?"

"Let's be honest, Mr. Rawlins. You are no carpenter."

He chuckled. She found herself wondering which had amused him more: her accusation or her refusal to use his Christian name.

"You have to give a feller a chance, Miss Aurora. You haven't even seen my handiwork yet."

"I take it you've worked on barns before?"

"Sure. Fences too. My older brothers have a ranch up near Bandera Pass. Zack raises cattle. Cord raises kids. I try to raise a little thunder now and then, but they won't let me." He winked. "That's why I had to ride south."

She felt a smile tug at her lips. She was inclined to believe a part of his story, the part about him rebelling against authority.

"You aren't gonna make me bed down again in these woods, are you, ma'am? 'Cause Two-Step is awful fond of hay."

He managed to look woeful, in spite of the impish humor lighting his eyes. She realized then just how practiced his roguery was. Wary again, she searched his gaze, trying to find some hint of the truth. Why hadn't he stayed at the hotel in town? Or worse, at the dance hall? She felt better knowing he hadn't spent his free time exploiting an unfortunate young whore, but she still worried that his reasons for sleeping alone had more to do with empty pockets than any nobility of character. What would Rawlins do if Dukker offered to hire his guns?

Maybe feeding and housing Rawlins was more prudent than driving him off. Boarding him could steer him away from Dukker's dangerous influence, and Shae could genuinely use the help on the barn.

"Very well, Mr. Rawlins. I shall withhold judgment on your carpentry skills until you've had a chance to prove yourself."

"Why, that's right kind of you, ma'am."

She felt her cheeks grow warm again. His lilting drawl had the all-too-disturbing tendency to make her feel uncertain and eighteen again.

"I suppose you'll want to ride on to the house now," she said. "It's a half-mile farther west. Shae is undoubtedly awake and can show you what to do." She inclined her head. "Good morning."

Except for a cannily raised eyebrow, he didn't budge.

Rorie fidgeted. She was unused to her dismissals going unheeded. She was especially unused to a young man regarding her as if she had just made the most delightful quip of the season.

Hoping he would go away if she ignored him, she stooped to retrieve her gun. He reached quickly to help. She was so stunned when he crouched before her, his corded thighs straining beneath the fabric of his blue jeans, that she leaped up, nearly butting her head against his. He chuckled.

"Do I make you nervous, ma'am?"

"Certainly not." Her ears burned at the lie. "Whatever makes you think that?"

"Well . . ." Still squatting, he scooped bullets out of the bluebonnets that rose like sapphire spears around her hem. "I was worried you might be trying to get rid of me again."

"I—I only thought that Shae was expecting you," she stammered, hastily backing away. There was something disconcerting—not to mention titillating—about a man's bronzed fingers snaking through the grass and darting so near to the unmentionables one wore beneath one's skirt.

"Shae's not expecting me yet, ma'am. The sun's too low in the sky." Rawlins straightened leisurely. "I figure I've got a half hour, maybe more, before I report to the barn. Just think, Miss Aurora, that gives us plenty of time to get acquainted."

On sale in September:

TAME THE WILD HEART
by Rosanne Bittner

BETROTHED
by Elizabeth Elliott

DON'T MISS THESE FABULOUS BANTAM WOMEN'S FICTION TITLES

On Sale in August

Available in mass market

AMANDA

from bestselling author *Kay Hooper*

"*Amanda* seethes and sizzles. A fast-paced atmospheric tale that vibrates with tension, passion, and mystery."

—CATHERINE COULTER

___ 56823-X $5.99/$7.99 Canada

THE MARSHAL AND THE HEIRESS

by *Patricia Potter*

"One of the romance genre's finest talents." —*Romantic Times*
The bestselling author of *Diablo* captivates with a western lawman lassoing the bad guys—in Scotland!___ 57508-2 $5.99/$7.99

from *Adrienne deWolfe*
the author *Romantic Times* touted as
"an exciting new talent" comes

TEXAS LOVER

Texas Ranger Wes Rawlins comes up against the barrel of a shotgun held by a beautiful Yankee woman with a gaggle of orphans under her care.   ___ 57481-7 $5.50/$7.50

Ask for these books at your local bookstore or use this page to order.

Please send me the books I have checked above. I am enclosing $___ (add $2.50 to cover postage and handling). Send check or money order, no cash or C.O.D.'s, please.

Name _____

Address _____

City/State/Zip _____

Send order to: Bantam Books, Dept. FN158, 2451 S. Wolf Rd., Des Plaines, IL 60018
Allow four to six weeks for delivery.
Prices and availability subject to change without notice.

FN 158 8/96

DON'T MISS THESE FABULOUS BANTAM WOMEN'S FICTION TITLES

On Sale in September

TAME THE WILD WIND

by ROSANNE BITTNER

the mistress of romantic frontier fiction

Here is the sweeping romance of a determined woman who runs a stagecoach inn and the half-breed who changes worlds to claim the woman he loves.

____ 56996-1 $5.99/$7.99 in Canada

BETROTHED

by ELIZABETH ELLIOTT

"An exciting find for romance readers everywhere!"
—AMANDA QUICK,
New York Times bestselling author

Guy of Montague rides into Lonsdale Castle to reclaim Halford Hall, only to be forced into a betrothal with the baron's beautiful niece.

____ 57566-X $5.50/$7.50 in Canada

Ask for these books at your local bookstore or use this page to order.

Please send me the books I have checked above. I am enclosing $____ (add $2.50 to cover postage and handling). Send check or money order, no cash or C.O.D.'s, please.

Name _____

Address _____

City/State/Zip _____

Send order to: Bantam Books, Dept. FN159, 2451 S. Wolf Rd., Des Plaines, IL 60018
Allow four to six weeks for delivery.
Prices and availability subject to change without notice.   FN 159 9/96